D0453400

GULLIVER'S TRAVELS

GULLIVER'S
TRAVELS

by

JONATHAN SWIFT

First printed in this edition in 1963
This edition published 1993 by
Diamond Books
77-85 Fulham Palace Road
Hammersmith, London, W6 8JB

Printed and bound in Great Britain by BPCC Hazells Ltd.

Contents

Travels into Several Remote Nations of the World

A LETTER

from Capt. Gulliver, to his
Cousin Sympson

I HOPE *you will be ready to own publickly, whenever you shall be called to it, that by your great and frequent Urgency you prevailed on me to publish a very loose and uncorrect Account of my Travels; with Direction to hire some young Gentleman of either University to put them in Order, and correct the Style, as my Cousin* Dampier *did by my Advice, in his Book called,* A Voyage round the World. *But I do not remember I gave you Power to consent, that any thing should be omitted, and much less that any thing should be inserted: Therefore, as to the latter, I do here renounce every thing of that Kind; particularly a Paragraph about her Majesty the late Queen* Anne, *of most pious and glorious Memory; although I did reverence and esteem her more than any of human Species. But you, or your Interpolator, ought to have considered, that as it was not my Inclination, so was it not decent to praise any Animal of our Composition before my Master* Houyhnhnm: *And besides, the Fact was altogether false; for to my Knowledge, being in* England *during some Part of her Majesty's Reign, she did govern by a chief Minister; nay, even by two successively; the first whereof was the Lord of* Godolphin, *and the second the Lord of* Oxford; *so that you have made me* say the thing that was not. *Likewise, in the Account of the Academy of Projectors, and several Passages of my Discourse to my Master* Houyhnhnm, *you have either omitted some material Circumstances, or minced or changed them in such a Manner, that I do hardly know mine own Work. When I formerly hinted to you something of this in a Letter, you were pleased to answer, that you were afraid of giving Offence; that People in Power were very watchful over the Press; and apt not only to interpret, but to punish every thing which looked like an* Inuendo (*as I think you called it.*) *But pray, how could that which I spoke so many Years ago, and at above five Thousand Leagues distance, in another*

Reign, be applyed to any of the Yahoos, who now are said to govern the Herd; especially, at a time when I little thought on or feared the Unhappiness of living under them. Have not I the most Reason to complain, when I see these very Yahoos carried by Houyhnhnms in a Vehicle, as if these were Brutes, and those the rational Creatures? And, indeed, to avoid so monstrous and detestable a Sight, was one principal Motive of my Retirement hither.

THUS much I thought proper to tell you in Relation to your self, and to the Trust I reposed in you.

I DO in the next Place complain of my own great Want of Judgment, in being prevailed upon by the Intreaties and false Reasonings of you and some others, very much against mine own Opinion, to suffer my Travels to be published. Pray bring to your Mind how often I desired you to consider, when you insisted on the Motive of publick Good; that the Yahoos were a Species of Animals utterly incapable of Amendment by Precepts or Examples: And so it hath proved; for instead of seeing a full Stop put to all Abuses and Corruptions, at least in this little Island, as I had Reason to expect: Behold, after above six Months Warning, I cannot learn that my Book hath produced one single Effect according to mine Intentions: I desired you would let me know by a Letter, when Party and Faction were extinguished; Judges learned and upright; Pleaders honest and modest, with some Tincture of common Sense; and Smithfield blazing with Pyramids of Law-Books; the young Nobility's Education entirely changed; the Physicians banished; the Female Yahoos abounding in Virtue, Honour, Truth and good Sense; Courts and Levees of great Ministers thoroughly weeded and swept; Wit, Merit and Learning rewarded; all Disgracers of the Press in Prose and Verse, condemned to eat nothing but their own Cotten, and quench their Thirst with their own Ink. These, and a Thousand other Reformations, I firmly counted upon by your Encouragement; as indeed they were plainly deducible from the Precepts delivered in my Book. And, it must be owned that seven Months were a sufficient Time to correct every Vice and Folly to which Yahoos are subject; if their Natures had been capable of the least Disposition to Virtue or Wisdom: Yet so far have you been from answering mine Expectation in any of your Letters; that on the contrary, you are

loading our Carrier every Week with Libels, and Keys, and
Reflections, and Memoirs, and Second Parts; wherein I see
myself accused of reflecting upon great States-Folk; of degrading
human Nature, (for so they have still the Confidence to stile it)
and of abusing the Female Sex. I find likewise, that the Writers
of those Bundles are not agreed among themselves; for some of
them will not allow me to be Author of mine own Travels; and
others make me Author of Books to which I am wholly a Stranger.

I FIND likewise, that your Printer hath been so careless as to
confound the Times, and mistake the Dates of my several Voyages
and Returns; neither assigning the true Year, or the true Month,
or Day of the Month: And I hear the original Manuscript is all
destroyed, since the Publication of my Book. Neither have I any
Copy left; however, I have sent you some Corrections, which you
may insert, if ever there should be a second Edition: And yet I
cannot stand to them, but shall leave that Matter to my judicious
and candid Readers, to adjust it as they please.

I HEAR some of our Sea-Yahoos find Fault with my Sea-
Language, as not proper in many Parts, nor now in Use. I cannot
help it. In my first Voyages, while I was young, I was instructed
by the oldest Mariners, and learned to speak as they did. But I
have since found that the Sea-Yahoos are apt, like the Land ones,
to become new fangled in their Words; which the latter change
every Year; insomuch, as I remember upon each Return to mine
own Country, their old Dialect was so altered, that I could hardly
understand the new. And I observe, when any Yahoo comes from
London out of Curiosity to visit me at mine own House, we
neither of us are able to deliver our Conceptions in a Manner
intelligible to the other.

IF the Censure of Yahoos could any Way affect me, I should
have great Reason to complain, that some of them are so bold as
to think my Book of Travels a meer Fiction out of mine own
Brain; and have gone so far as to drop Hints, that the Houy-
hnhnms, and Yahoos have no more Existence than the Inhabitants
of Utopia.

INDEED I must confess, that as to the People of Lilliput,
Brobdingrag, (for so the Word should have been spelt, and not
erroneously Brobdingnag) and Laputa; I have never yet heard
of any Yahoo so presumptuous as to dispute their Being, or the

Facts I have related concerning them; because the Truth immediately strikes every Reader with Conviction. And, is there less Probability in my Account of the Houyhnhnms or Yahoos, when it is manifest as to the latter, there are so many Thousands even in this City, who only differ from their Brother Brutes in Houyhnhnmland, because they use a Sort of a Jabber, and do not go naked. I wrote for their Amendment, and not their Approbation. The united Praise of the whole Race would be of less Consequence to me, than the neighing of those two degenerate Houyhnhnms I keep in my Stable; because, from these, degenerate as they are, I still improve in some Virtues, without any Mixture of Vice.

DO these miserable Animals presume to think that I am so far degenerated as to defend my Veracity; Yahoo as I am, it is well known through all Houyhnhnmland, that by the Instructions and Example of my illustrious Master, I was able in the Compass of two Years (although I confess with the utmost Difficulty) to remove that infernal Habit of Lying, Shuffling, Deceiving, and Equivocating, so deeply rooted in the very Souls of all my Species; especially the Europeans.

I HAVE other Complaints to make upon this vexatious Occasion; but I forbear troubling myself on you any further. I must freely confess, that since my last Return, some Corruptions of my Yahoo Nature have revived in me by conversing with a few of your Species, and particularly those of mine own Family, by an unavoidable Necessity; else I should never have attempted so absurd a Project as that of reforming the Yahoo Race in this Kingdom; but, I have now done with all such visionary Schemes for ever.

April 2, 1727

THE PUBLISHER TO
THE READER

THE AUTHOR *of these Travels, Mr.* Lemuel Gulliver, *is my antient and intimate Friend; there is likewise some Relation between us by the Mother's Side. About three Years ago Mr.* Gulliver *growing weary of the Concourse of curious People coming to him at his House in* Redriff, *made a small Purchase of Land, with a convenient House, near* Newark, *in* Nottinghamshire, *his native Country; where he now lives retired, yet in good Esteem among his Neighbours.*

ALTHOUGH *Mr.* Gulliver *were born in* Nottinghamshire, *where his Father dwelt, yet I have heard him say, his Family came from* Oxfordshire; *to confirm which, I have observed in the Church-Yard at* Banbury, *in that County, several Tombs and Monuments of the* Gullivers.

BEFORE *he quitted* Redriff, *he left the Custody of the following Papers in my Hands, with the Liberty to dispose of them as I should think fit. I have carefully perused them three Times; The Style is very plain and simple; and the only Fault I find is, that the Author, after the Manner of Travellers, is a little too circumstantial. There is an Air of Truth apparent through the whole; and indeed the Author was so distinguished for his Veracity, that it became a Sort of Proverb among his Neighbours at* Redriff, *when anyone affirmed a Thing, to say, it was as true as if Mr.* Gulliver *had spoke it.*

BY *the Advice of several worthy Persons, to whom, with the Author's Permission, I communicated these Papers, I now venture to send them into the World; hoping they may be, at least for some time, a better Entertainment to our young Noblemen, than the common Scribbles of Politicks and Party.*

THIS *Volume would have been at least twice as large, if I had not made bold to strike out innumerable Passages relating to the Winds and Tides, as well as to the Variations and Bearings in the several Voyages; together with the minute Descriptions of the Management of the Ship in Storms, in the Style of Sailors:*

15

Likewise the Account of the Longitudes and Latitudes; wherein I have Reason to apprehend that Mr. Gulliver may be a little dissatisfied: But I was resolved to fit the Work as much as possible to the general Capacity of Readers. However, if my own Ignorance in Sea-Affairs shall have led me to commit some Mistakes, I alone am answerable for them: And if any Traveller hath a Curiosity to see the whole Work at large, as it came from the Hand of the Author, I will be ready to gratify him.

As for any further Particulars relating to the Author, the Reader will receive Satisfaction from the first Pages of the Book.

RICHARD SYMPSON

PART ONE

A VOYAGE TO LILLIPUT

CHAPTER ONE

THE AUTHOR GIVETH SOME ACCOUNT OF HIMSELF AND FAMILY;
HIS FIRST INDUCEMENTS TO TRAVEL. HE IS SHIPWRECKED, AND
SWIMS FOR HIS LIFE; GETS SAFE ON SHOAR IN THE COUNTRY OF
LILLIPUT; IS MADE A PRISONER, AND CARRIED UP THE COUNTRY.

My Father had a small Estate in *Nottinghamshire*; I was
the Third of five Sons. He sent me to *Emanuel-College*
in *Cambridge*, at Fourteen Years old, where I resided three
Years, and applied my self close to my Studies: But the Charge
of maintaining me (although I had a very scanty Allowance)
being too great for a narrow Fortune; I was bound Apprentice
to Mr. *James Bates*, an eminent Surgeon in *London*, with whom
I continued four Years; and my Father now and then sending
me small Sums of Money, I laid them out in learning Navigation and other Parts of the Mathematicks, useful to those who
intend to travel, as I always believed it would be some time or
other my Fortune to do. When I left Mr. *Bates*, I went down
to my Father; where, by the Assistance of him and my Uncle
John, and some other Relations, I got Forty Pounds, and a
Promise of Thirty Pounds a Year to maintain me at *Leyden*:
There I studied Physick two Years and seven Months, knowing
it would be useful in long Voyages.

Soon after my return from *Leyden*, I was recommended by
my good Master Mr. *Bates*, to be Surgeon to the *Swallow*,
Captain *Abraham Pannell* Commander; with whom I continued three Years and a half, making a Voyage or two into the
Levant and some other Parts. When I came back, I resolved
to settle in *London*, to which Mr. *Bates*, my Master, encouraged
me; and by him I was recommended to several Patients. I
took Part of a small House in the *Old Jury*; and being advised

to alter my Condition, I married Mrs. *Mary Burton*, second Daughter to Mr. *Edmond Burton*, Hosier, in *Newgate-street*, with whom I received four Hundred Pounds for a Portion.

But, my good Master *Bates* dying in two Years after, and I having few Friends my Business began to fail; for my Conscience would not suffer me to imitate the bad Practice of too many among my Brethren. Having therefore consulted with my Wife, and some of my acquaintance, I determined to go again to Sea. I was Surgeon successively in two Ships, and made Several Voyages, for six Years, to the *East* and *West-Indies*; by which I got some Addition to my Fortune. My Hours of Leisure I spent in reading the best Authors, ancient and modern; being always provided with a good Number of Books; and when I was ashore, in observing the Manners and Dispositions of the People, as well as learning their Language; wherein I had a great Facility by the Strength of my Memory.

The last of these Voyages not proving very fortunate, I grew weary of the Sea, and intended to stay at home with my Wife and Family. I removed from the *Old Jury* to *Fetter Lane*, and from thence to *Wapping*, hoping to get Business among the Sailors; but it would not turn to account. After three Years Expectation that things would mend, I accepted an advantageous Offer from Captain *William Prichard*, Master of the *Antelope*, who was making a Voyage to the *South-Sea*. We set sail from *Bristol*, *May* 4th, 1699, and our Voyage at first was very prosperous.

It would not be proper for some Reasons, to trouble the Reader with the Particulars of our Adventures in those Seas: Let it suffice to inform him, that in our Passage from thence to the *East-Indies*, we were driven by a violent Storm to the North-west of *Van Diemen's* Land. By an Observation, we found ourselves in the Latitude of 30 Degrees 2 Minutes South. Twelve of our Crew were dead by immoderate Labour, and ill Food; the rest were in a very weak Condition. On the fifth of *November*, which was the beginning of Summer in those Parts, the Weather being very hazy, the Seamen spyed a Rock, within half a Cable's length of the Ship; but the Wind was so strong, that we were driven directly upon it, and immediately split. Six of the Crew, of whom I was one, having let down the

Boat into the Sea, made a Shift to get clear of the Ship, and the Rock. We rowed by my Computation, about three Leagues, till we were able to work no longer, being already spent with Labour while we were in the Ship. We therefore trusted ourselves to the Mercy of the Waves; and in about half an Hour the Boat was overset by a sudden Flurry from the North. What became of my Companions in the Boat, as well as of those who escaped on the Rock, or were left in the Vessel, I cannot tell; but conclude they were all lost. For my own Part, I swam as Fortune directed me, and was pushed forward by Wind and Tide. I often let my Legs drop, and could feel no Bottom; But when I was almost gone, and able to struggle no longer, I found myself within my Depth; and by this Time the Storm was much abated. The Declivity was so small, that I walked near a Mile before I got to the Shore, which I conjectured was about Eight o'Clock in the Evening. I then advanced forward near half a Mile, but could not discover any Sign of Houses or Inhabitants; at least I was in so weak a Condition, that I did not observe them. I was extremely tired, and with that, and the Heat of the Weather, and about half a Pint of Brandy that I drank as I left the Ship, I found my self much inclined to sleep. I lay down on the Grass, which was very short and soft; where I slept sounder than ever I remember to have done in my Life, and as I reckoned, above Nine Hours; for when I awaked, it was just Day-light. I attempted to rise, but was not able to stir: For as I happened to lie on my Back, I found my Arms and Legs were strongly fastened on each Side to the Ground; and my Hair, which was long and thick, tied down in the same Manner. I likewise felt several slender Ligatures across my Body, from my Armpits to my Thighs. I could only look upwards; the Sun began to grow hot, and the Light offended my Eyes. I heard a confused Noise about me, but in the Posture I lay, could see nothing except the Sky. In a little time I felt something alive and moving on my left Leg, which advancing gently forward over my Breast, came almost up to my Chin; when bending my Eyes downwards as much as I could, I perceived it to be a human Creature not six Inches high, with a Bow and Arrow in his Hands, and a Quiver at his Back. In the mean time, I felt at least Forty more of the same Kind (as I conjectured) following the first. I was in the utmost Astonishment, and roared so loud, that they all ran back in a Fright ; and some of them, as I was afterwards told, were hurt with the Falls they got by leaping from my Sides upon the Ground. However, they soon returned ; and one of them, who ventured so far as to get a full Sight of my Face, lifting up his Hands and Eyes by way of Admiration, cryed out in a shrill, but distinct Voice, *Hekinah Degul*: The others repeated the same Words several times, but I then knew not what they meant. I lay all this while, as the Reader may believe, in great Uneasiness ; At length, struggling to get loose, I had the Fortune to break the Strings, and wrench out the Pegs that fastened my left Arm to the Ground ; for, by lifting it up to my Face, I discovered the Methods they had taken to bind me ; and, at the same time, with a violent Pull, which gave me excessive Pain, I a little loosened the Strings that tied down my Hair on the left Side ; so that I was just able to turn my Head about two Inches. But the Creatures ran off a second time, before I could seize them ; whereupon there was a great Shout in a very shrill Accent ; and after it ceased, I heard one of them cry aloud, *Tolgo Phonac* ; when in an Instant I felt above an Hundred Arrows discharged on my left Hand, which pricked me like so many Needles ; and besides, they shot another Flight into the Air, as we do Bombs in *Europe* ; whereof many, I suppose, fell on my Body, (though I felt them not) and some on my Face, which I immediately covered with my left Hand. When this Shower of Arrows was over, I fell a groaning with Grief and Pain ; and then striving again to get loose, they discharged another Volley larger than the first ; and some of them attempted with Spears to stick me in the Sides ; but by good Luck, I had on me a Buff Jerkin, which they could not pierce. I thought it the most prudent Method to lie still ; and my Design was to continue so till Night, when my left Hand being already loose, I could easily free myself : And as for the Inhabitants, I had Reason to believe I might be a Match for the greatest Armies they could bring against me, if they were all of the same Size with him that I saw. But Fortune disposed otherwise of me. When the People observed I was quiet, they discharged no more Arrows : But by the Noise increasing, I knew their Numbers were greater; and about four Yards from me, over-against my right Ear, I heard a Knocking for above an Hour, like People at work; when turning my Head that Way, as well as the Pegs and Strings would permit me, I saw a Stage erected about a Foot and a half from the Ground, capable of holding four of the Inhabitants, with two or three Ladders to mount it : From whence one of them, who seemed to be a Person of Quality, made me a long Speech, whereof I understood not one Syllable. But I should have mentioned, that before the principal Person began his Oration, he cryed out three times *Langro Dehul san* : (these Words and the former were afterwards repeated and explained to me.) Whereupon immediately about fifty of the Inhabitants came, and cut the Strings that fastened the left side of my Head, which gave me the Liberty of turning it to the right, and of observing the Person and Gesture of him who was to speak. He appeared to be of a middle Age, and taller than any of the other three who attended him; whereof one was a Page, who held up his Train, and seemed to be somewhat longer than my middle Finger; the other two stood on each side to support him. He acted every part of an Orator; and I could observe many Periods of Threatenings, and others of Promises, Pity and Kindness. I answered in a few Words, but in the most submissive Manner, lifting up my left Hand and both my eyes to the Sun, as calling him for a Witness; and being almost famished with Hunger, having not eaten a Morsel for some Hours before I left the Ship, I found the Demands of Nature so strong upon me, that I could not forbear shewing my Impatience (perhaps against the strict Rules of Decency) by putting my Finger frequently on my Mouth, to signify that I wanted Food. The *Hurgo* (for so they called a great Lord, as I afterwards learnt) understood me very well : He descended from the Stage, and commanded that several Ladders should be applied to my Sides, on which above an hundred of the Inhabitants mounted, and walked towards my Mouth laden with Baskets full of Meat, which had been provided and sent thither by the King's Orders upon the first Intelligence he received of me. I observed there was the Flesh of several Animals, but could not distinguish them by the Taste. There were Shoulders, Legs, and Loins shaped like those of Mutton, and very well dressed, but smaller than the Wings of a Lark. I ate them by two or three at a Mouthful; and took three Loaves at a time, about the bigness of Musket Bullets. They supplyed me as fast as they could, shewing a thousand Marks of Wonder and Astonishment at my Bulk and Appetite. I then made another Sign that I wanted Drink. They found by my eating that a small Quantity would not suffice me; and being a most ingenious People, they slung up with great Dexterity one of their largest Hogsheads; then rolled it towards my Hand, and beat out the Top; I drank it off at a Draught, which I might well do, for it hardly held half a Pint, and tasted like a small Wine of *Burgundy*, but much more delicious. They brought me a second Hogshead, which I drank in the same Manner, and made Signs for more, but they had none to give me. When I had performed these Wonders, they shouted for Joy, and danced upon my Breast, repeating several times as they did at first, *Hekinah Degul*. They made me a Sign that I should throw down the two Hogsheads, but first warned the People below to stand out of the Way, crying aloud, *Borach Mivola*; and when they saw the Vessels in the Air, there was an universal Shout of *Hekinah Degul*. I confess I was often tempted, while they were passing backwards and forwards on my Body, to seize Forty or Fifty of the first that came in my Reach and dash them against the Ground. But the Remembrance of what I had felt, which probably might not be the worst they could do; and the Promise of Honour I made them, for so I interpreted my submissive Behaviour, soon drove out those Imaginations. Besides, I now considered my self as bound by the Laws of Hospitality to a People who had treated me with so much Expence and Magnificence. However in my Thoughts I could not sufficiently wonder at the Intrepidity of these diminutive Mortals, who durst venture to mount and walk on my Body, while one of my Hands was at Liberty, without trembling at the very Sight of so prodigious a Creature as I must appear to them. After some time, when they observed that I made no more Demands for Meat, there appeared before me a Person of high Rank from his Imperial Majesty. His Excellency having mounted on the Small of my Right Leg,

advanced forwards up to my Face, with about a Dozen of his
Retinue; And producing his Credentials under the Signet
Royal, which he applied close to my Eyes, spoke about ten
Minutes, without any Signs of Anger, but with a kind of
determinate Resolution; often pointing forwards, which, as I
afterwards found, was towards the Capital City, about half a
Mile distant, whither it was agreed by his Majesty in Council
that I must be conveyed. I answered in few Words, but to no
Purpose, and made a Sign with my Hand that was loose,
putting it to the other, (but over his Excellency's Head, for
Fear of hurting him or his Train) and then to my own Head
and Body, to signify that I desired my Liberty. It appeared
that he understood me well enough; for he shook his Head by
way of Disapprobation, and held his Hand in a Posture to shew
that I must be carried as a Prisoner. However, he made other
Signs to let me understand that I should have Meat and Drink
enough, and very good Treatment. Whereupon I once more
thought of attempting to break my Bonds; but again, when I
felt the Smart of their Arrows upon my Face and Hands, which
were all in Blisters, and many of the Darts still sticking in them;
and observing likewise that the Number of my Enemies
encreased; I gave Tokens to let them know that they might
do with me what they pleased. Upon this, the *Hurgo* and his
Train withdrew, with much Civility and chearful Countenances.
Soon after I heard a general Shout, with frequent Repetitions
of the Words, *Peplom Selan*, and I felt great Numbers of the
People on my Left Side relaxing the Cords to such a Degree,
that I was able to turn upon my Right. But before this, they
had dawbed my Face and both my Hands with a sort of Ointment very pleasant to the Smell, which in a few Minutes
removed all the Smart of their Arrows. These Circumstances,
added to the Refreshment I had received by their Victuals and
Drink, which were very nourishing, disposed me to sleep. I
slept about eight Hours as I was afterwards assured; and it
was no Wonder; for the Physicians, by the Emperor's Order,
had mingled a Sleeping Potion in the Hogsheads of Wine.

It seems that upon the first Moment I was discovered sleeping
on the Ground after my Landing, the Emperor had early
Notice of it by an Express; and determined in Council that

I should be tyed in the Manner I have related, (which was done in the Night while I slept) that Plenty of Meat and Drink should be sent me, and a Machine prepared to carry me to the Capital City.

This Resolution perhaps may appear very bold and dangerous, and I am confident would not be imitated by any Prince in *Europe* on the like Occasion; however, in my Opinion it was extremely Prudent as well as Generous. For supposing these People had endeavoured to kill me with their Spears and Arrows while I was asleep; I should certainly have awaked with the first Sense of Smart, which might so far have rouzed my Rage and Strength, as to enable me to break the Strings wherewith I was tyed; after which, as they were not able to make Resistance, so they could expect no Mercy.

These People are the most excellent Mathematicians, and arrived to a great Perfection in Mechanicks by the Countenance and Encouragement of the Emperor, who is a renowned Patron of Learning. This Prince hath several Machines fixed on Wheels, for the Carriage of Trees and other great Weights. He often buildeth his largest Men of War, whereof some are Nine Foot long, in the Woods where the Timber grows, and has them carried on these Engines three or four Hundred Yards to the Sea. Five Hundred Carpenters and Engineers were immediately set at work to prepare the greatest Engine they had. It was a Frame of Wood raised three Inches from the Ground, about seven Foot long and four wide, moving upon twenty-two Wheels. The Shout I heard, was upon the Arrival of this Engine, which, it seems, set out in four Hours after my Landing. It was brought parallel to me as I lay. But the principal Difficulty was to raise and place me in this Vehicle. Eighty Poles, each of one Foot high, were erected for this Purpose, and very strong Cords of the bigness of Pack thread were fastened by Hooks to many Bandages, which the Workmen had girt round my Neck, my Hands, my Body, and my Legs. Nine Hundred of the strongest Men were employed to draw up these Cords by many Pullies fastened on the Poles; and thus in less than three Hours, I was raised and slung into the Engine, and there tyed fast. All this I was told; for while the whole Operation was performing, I lay in a profound Sleep, by the Force of that soporiferous Medicine infused into my Liquor. Fifteen hundred of the Emperor's largest Horses, each about four Inches and a half high, were employed to draw me towards the Metropolis, which, as I said, was half a Mile distant.

About four Hours after we began our Journey, I awaked by a very ridiculous Accident; for the Carriage being stopt a while to adjust something that was out of Order, two or three of the young Natives had the Curiosity to see how I looked when I was asleep; they climbed up into the Engine, and advancing very softly to my Face, one of them, an Officer in the Guards, put the sharp End of his Half-Pike a good way up into my left Nostril, which tickled my Nose like a Straw, and made me sneeze violently: Whereupon they stole off unperceived; and it was three Weeks before I knew the Cause of my awaking so suddenly. We made a long March the remaining Part of the Day, and rested at Night with Five Hundred Guards on each Side of me, half with Torches, and half with Bows and Arrows, ready to shoot me if I should offer to stir. The next Morning at Sunrise we continued our March, and arrived within two Hundred Yards of the City-Gates about Noon. The Emperor, and all his Court, came out to meet us; but his great Officers would by no Means suffer his Majesty to endanger his Person by mounting on my Body.

At the Place where the Carriage stopt, there stood an ancient Temple, esteemed to be the largest in the whole Kingdom; which having been polluted some Years before by an unnatural Murder, was, according to the Zeal of those People, looked upon as Prophane, and therefore had been applied to common Uses, and all the Ornaments and Furniture carried away. In this Edifice it was determined I should lodge. The great Gate fronting to the North was about four Foot high, and almost two Foot wide, through which I could easily creep. On each Side of the Gate was a small Window not above six Inches from the Ground: Into that on the Left Side, the King's Smiths conveyed fourscore and eleven Chains, like those that hang to a Lady's Watch in *Europe*, and almost as large, which were locked to my Left Leg with six and thirty Padlocks. Over against this Temple, on the other Side of the great Highway,

at twenty Foot Distance, there was a Turret at least five Foot
high. Here the Emperor ascended with many principal Lords
of his Court, to have an Opportunity of viewing me, as I was
told, for I could not see them. It was reckoned that above an
hundred thousand Inhabitants came out of the Town upon
the same Errand; and in spight of my Guards, I believe there
could not be fewer than ten thousand, at several Times, who
mounted upon my Body by the Help of Ladders. But a
Proclamation was soon issued to forbid it, upon Pain of Death.
When the Workmen found it was impossible for me to break
loose, they cut all the Strings that bound me; whereupon I
rose up with as melancholy a Disposition as ever I had in my
Life. But the Noise and Astonishment of the People at seeing
me rise and walk, are not to be expressed. The Chains that
held my left Leg were about two Yards long, and gave me not
only the Liberty of walking backwards and forwards in a
Semicircle; but being fixed within four Inches of the Gate,
allowed me to creep in, and lie at my full Length in the Temple.

CHAPTER TWO

THE EMPEROR OF LILLIPUT, ATTENDED BY SEVERAL OF THE
NOBILITY, COMES TO SEE THE AUTHOR IN HIS CONFINEMENT. THE
EMPEROR'S PERSON AND HABIT DESCRIBED. LEARNED MEN AP-
POINTED TO TEACH THE AUTHOR THEIR LANGUAGE. HE GAINS
FAVOUR BY HIS MILD DISPOSITION. HIS POCKETS ARE SEARCHED,
AND HIS SWORD AND PISTOLS TAKEN FROM HIM.

WHEN I found myself on my Feet, I looked about me,
and must confess I never beheld a more entertaining
Prospect. The Country round appeared like a continued
Garden; and the inclosed Fields, which were generally Forty
Foot square, resembled so many Beds of Flowers. These
Fields were intermingled with Woods of half a Stang, and the
tallest Trees, as I could judge, appeared to be seven Foot high.
I viewed the Town on my left Hand, which looked like the
painted Scene of a City in a Theatre.

The Emperor was already descended from the Tower, and advancing on Horseback towards me, which had like to have cost him dear; for the Beast, although very well trained, yet wholly unused to such a Sight, which appeared as if a Mountain moved before him, reared up on his hinder Feet: But that Prince, who is an excellent Horseman, kept his Seat, until his Attendants ran in, and held the Bridle, while his Majesty had Time to dismount. When he alighted, he surveyed me round with great Admiration, but kept beyond the Length of my Chains. He ordered his Cooks and Butlers, who were already prepared, to give me Victuals and Drink, which they pushed forward in a sort of Vehicles upon Wheels until I could reach them. I took these Vehicles, and soon emptied them all; twenty of them were filled with Meat, and ten with Liquor; each of the former afforded me two or three good Mouthfuls, and I emptied the Liquor of ten Vessels, which was contained in earthen Vials into one Vehicle, drinking it off at a Draught; and so I did with the rest. The Empress, and young Princes of the Blood, of both Sexes, attended by many Ladies, sate at some Distance in their Chairs; but upon the Accident that happened to the Emperor's Horse, they alighted, and came near his Person; which I am now going to describe. He is taller by almost the Breadth of my Nail, than any of his Court; which alone is enough to strike an Awe into the Beholders. His Features are strong and masculine, with an *Austrian* Lip, and arched Nose, his Complexion olive, his Countenance erect, his Body and Limbs well proportioned, all his Motions graceful, and his Deportment majestick. For the better Convenience of beholding him, I lay on my Side, so that my Face was parallel to his, and he stood but three Yards off; However, I have had him since many Times in my Hand, and therefore cannot be deceived in the Description. His Dress was very plain and simple, the Fashion of it between the *Asiatick* and the *European*; but he had on his Head a light Helmet of Gold, adorned with Jewels, and a Plume on the Crest. He held his Sword drawn in his Hand, to defend himself, if I should happen to break loose; it was almost three Inches long, the Hilt and Scabbard were Gold enriched with Diamonds. His Voice was shrill, but very clear and articulate, and I could distinctly hear it when I stood up. The Ladies and Courtiers were all most magnificently clad, so that the Spot they stood upon seemed to resemble a Petticoat spread on the Ground, embroidered with Figures of Gold and Silver. His Imperial Majesty spoke often to me, and I returned Answers, but neither of us could understand a Syllable. There were several of his Priests and Lawyers present (as I conjectured by their Habits) who were commanded to address themselves to me, and I spoke to them in as many Languages as I had the least Smattering of, which were *High* and *Low Dutch, Latin, French, Spanish, Italian,* and *Lingua Franca*; but all to no purpose. After about two Hours the Court retired, and I was left with a strong Guard, to prevent the Impertinence, and probably the Malice of the Rabble, who were very impatient to croud about me as near as they durst; and some of them had the Impudence to shoot their Arrows at me as I sate on the Ground by the Door of my House; whereof one very narrowly missed my left Eye. But the Colonel ordered six of the Ringleaders to be seized, and thought no Punishment so proper as to deliver them bound into my Hands, which some of his Soldiers accordingly did, pushing them forwards with the But-ends of their Pikes into my Reach : I took them all in my right Hand, put five of them into my Coat-pocket; and as to the sixth, I made a Countenance as if I would eat him alive. The poor Man squalled terribly, and the Colonel and his Officers were in much Pain, especially when they saw me take out my Penknife : But I soon put them out of Fear; for, looking mildly, and immediately cutting the Strings he was bound with, I set him gently on the Ground, and away he ran. I treated the rest in the same Manner, taking them one by one out of my Pocket; and I observed, both the Soldiers and the People were highly obliged at this Mark of my Clemency, which was represented very much to my Advantage at Court.

Towards Night I got with some Difficulty into my House, where I lay on the Ground, and continued to do so about a Fortnight; during which time the Emperor gave Orders to have a Bed prepared for me. Six Hundred Beds of the common Measure were brought in Carriages, and worked up into my House; an Hundred and Fifty of their Beds sown together made up the Breadth and Length, and these were four double, which however kept me but very indifferently from the Hardness of the Floor, that was of smooth Stone. By the same Computation they provided me with Sheets, Blankets, and Coverlets, tolerable enough for one who had been so long enured to Hardships as I.

As the News of my Arrival spread through the kingdom, it brought prodigious Numbers of rich, idle, and curious People to see me; so that the Villages were almost emptied, and great Neglect of Tillage and Houshold Affairs must have ensued, if his Imperial Majesty had not provided by several Proclamations and Orders of State against this Inconveniency. He directed that those, who had already beheld me, should return home, and not presume to come within fifty Yards of my House, without Licence from Court; whereby the Secretaries of State got considerable Fees.

In the mean time, the Emperor held frequent Councils to debate what Course should be taken with me; and I was afterwards assured by a particular Friend, a Person of great Quality, and who was as much in the *Secret* as any; that the Court was under many Difficulties concerning me. They apprehended my breaking loose; that my Diet would be very expensive, and might cause a Famine. Sometimes they determined to starve me, or at least to shoot me in the Face and Hands with poisoned Arrows, which would soon dispatch me: But again they considered, that the Stench of so large a Carcase might produce a Plague in the Metropolis, and probably spread through the whole Kingdom. In the midst of these Consultations, several Officers of the Army went to the Door of the great Council Chamber; and two of them being admitted, gave an Account of my Behaviour to the six Criminals abovementioned; which made so favourable an Impression in the Breast of his Majesty, and the whole Board, in my Behalf, that an Imperial Commission was issued out, obliging all the Villages nine hundred Yards round the City, to deliver in every Morning six Beeves, forty Sheep, and other Victuals for my Sustenance; together with a proportionable Quantity of Bread and Wine, and other Liquors: For the due Payment of which his Majesty gave Assignments upon his Treasury. For this

Prince lives chiefly upon his own Demesnes; seldom, except upon great Occasions raising any Subsidies upon his Subjects, who are bound to attend him in his Wars at their own Expence. An Establishment was also made of Six Hundred Persons to be my Domesticks, who had Board-Wages allowed for their Maintenance, and Tents built for them very conveniently on each side of my Door. It was likewise ordered, that three hundred Taylors should make me a Suit of Cloaths after the Fashion of the Country: That, six of his Majesty's greatest Scholars should be employed to instruct me in their Language: And, lastly, that the Emperor's Horses, and those of the Nobility, and Troops of Guards, should be exercised in my Sight, to accustom themselves to me. All these Orders were duly put in Execution; and in about three Weeks I made a great Progress in Learning their Language; during which Time the Emperor frequently honoured me with his Visits, and was pleased to assist my Masters in teaching me. We began already to converse together in some Sort; and the first Words I learnt, were to express my Desire, that he would please to give me my Liberty; which I every Day repeated on my Knees. His Answer, as I could apprehend, was, that this must be a Work of Time, not to be thought on without the Advice of his Council; and that first I must *Lumos Kelmin pesso desmar lon Emposo*; that is, *Swear a Peace with him and his Kingdom.* However, that I should be used with all Kindness; and he advised me to acquire by my Patience and discreet Behaviour, the good Opinion of himself and his Subjects. He desired I would not take it ill, if he gave Orders to certain proper Officers to search me; for probably I might carry about me several Weapons, which must needs be dangerous Things, if they answered the Bulk of so prodigious a Person. I said, his Majesty should be satisfied, for I was ready to strip my self, and turn up my Pockets before him. This I delivered, part in Words, and part in Signs. He replied, that by the Laws of the Kingdom, I must be searched by two of his Officers: That he knew this could not be done without my Consent and Assistance; that he had so good an Opinion of my Generosity and Justice, as to trust their Persons in my Hands: That whatever they took from me should be returned when I left the Country, or paid for at the Rate which I would set upon them. I took up the two Officers in my Hands, put them first into my Coat-Pockets, and then into every other Pocket about me, except my two Fobs, and another secret Pocket which I had no Mind should be searched, wherein I had some little Necessaries of no Consequence to any but my self. In one of my Fobs there was a Silver Watch, and in the other a small Quantity of Gold in a Purse. These Gentlemen, having Pen, Ink, and Paper about them, made an exact Inventory of every thing they saw; and when they had done, desired I would set them down, that they might deliver it to the Emperor. This Inventory I afterwards translated into *English*, and is Word for Word as follows.

Imprimis, In the right Coat-Pocket of the *Great Man Mountain* (for so I interpret the Words *Quinbus Flestrin*) after the strictest Search, we found only one great Piece of coarse Cloth, large enough to be a Foot-Cloth for your Majesty's chief Room of State. In the left Pocket, we saw a huge Silver Chest, with a Cover of the same Metal, which we, the Searchers, were not able to lift. We desired it should be opened; and one of us stepping into it, found himself up to the mid Leg in a sort of Dust, some part whereof flying up to our Faces, set us both a sneezing for several Times together. In his right Waistcoat-Pocket, we found a prodigious Bundle of white thin Substances, folded one over another, about the Bigness of three Men, tied with a strong Cable, and marked with black Figures; which we humbly conceive to be Writings; every Letter almost half as large as the Palm of our Hands. In the left there was a sort of Engine, from the Back of which were extended twenty long Poles, resembling the Pallisado's before your Majesty's Court; wherewith we conjecture the *Man Mountain* combs his Head; for we did not always trouble him with Questions, because we found it a great Difficulty to make him understand us. In the large Pocket on the right Side of his middle Cover, (so I translate the Word *Ranfu-Lo*, by which they meant my Breeches) we saw a hollow Pillar of Iron, about the Length of a Man, fastened to a strong Piece of Timber, larger than the Pillar; and upon one side of the Pillar were huge Pieces of Iron sticking out, cut into strange Figures;

which we know not what to make of. In the left Pocket,
another Engine of the same kind. In the smaller Pocket on the
right Side, were several round flat Pieces of white and red Metal,
of different Bulk : Some of the white, which seemed to be
Silver, were so large and heavy, that my Comrade and I could
hardly lift them. In the left Pocket were two black Pillars
irregularly shaped : we could not, without Difficulty, reach the
Top of them as we stood at the Bottom of his Pocket : One of
them was covered, and seemed all of a Piece ; but at the upper
End of the other, there appeared a white round Substance,
about twice the bigness of our Heads. Within each of these was
inclosed a prodigious Plate of Steel ; which, by our Orders, we
obliged him to shew us, because we apprehended they might
be dangerous Engines. He took them out of their Cases, and
told us, that in his own Country his Practice was to shave his
Beard with one of these, and to cut his Meat with the other.
There were two Pockets which we could not enter : These he
called his Fobs ; they were two large Slits cut into the Top of
his middle Cover, but squeezed close by the Pressure of his
Belly. Out of the right Fob hung a great Silver Chain, with a
wonderful kind of Engine at the Bottom. We directed him to
draw out whatever was at the End of that Chain ; which
appeared to be a Globe, half Silver, and half of some transparent
Metal : For on the transparent Side we saw certain strange
Figures circularly drawn, and thought we could touch them,
until we found our Fingers stopped with that lucid Substance.
He put this Engine to our Ears, which made an incessant Noise
like that of a Water-Mill. And we conjecture it is either some
unknown Animal, or the God that he worships : But we are
more inclined to the latter Opinion, because he assured us (if
we understood him right, for he expressed himself very im-
perfectly) that he seldom did any Thing without consulting it.
He called it his Oracle, and said it pointed out the Time for
every Action of his Life. From the left Fob he took out a Net
almost large enough for a Fisherman, but contrived to open and
shut like a Purse, and served him for the same Use : We found
therein several massy Pieces of yellow Metal, which if they be of
real Gold, must be of immense Value.

Having thus, in Obedience to your Majesty's Commands,

diligently searched all his Pockets ; we observed a Girdle about his Waist made of the Hyde of some prodigious Animal ; from which, on the Left Side, hung a Sword of the Length of five Men ; and on the right, a Bag or Pouch divided into two Cells ; each Cell capable of holding three of your Majesty's Subjects. In one of these Cells were several Globes or Balls of a most ponderous Metal, about the Bigness of our Heads, and required a strong Hand to lift them : The other Cell contained a Heap of certain black Grains, but of no great Bulk or Weight, for we could hold about fifty of them in the Palms of our Hands.

This is an exact Inventory of what we found about the Body of the *Man Mountain* ; who used us with great Civility, and due Respect to your Majesty's Commission. Signed and Sealed on the fourth Day of the eighty ninth Moon of your Majesty's auspicious Reign.

Clefren Frelock, Marsi Frelock.

When the Inventory was read over to the Emperor, he directed me to deliver up the several Particulars. He first called for my Scymiter, which I took out, Scabbard and all. In the mean time he ordered three thousand of his choicest Troops, who then attended him, to surround me at a Distance, with their Bows and Arrows just ready to discharge : But I did not observe it ; for my Eyes were wholly fixed upon his Majesty. He then desired me to draw my Scymiter, which, although it had got some Rust by the Sea-Water, was in most Parts exceeding bright. I did so, and immediately all the Troops gave a Shout between Terror and Surprize ; for the Sun shone clear, and the Reflexion dazzled their Eyes, as I waved the Scymiter to and fro in my Hand. His Majesty who is a most magnanimous Prince, was less daunted than I could expect ; he ordered me to return it into the Scabbard, and cast it on the Ground as gently as I could, about six Foot from the End of my Chain. The next Thing he demanded was one of the hollow Iron Pillars, by which he meant my Pocket-Pistols. I drew it out, and at his Desire, as well as I could, expressed to him the Use of it, and charging it only with Powder, which by the Closeness of my Pouch, happened to escape wetting in the

Sea, I first cautioned the Emperor not to be afraid; and then I let it off in the Air. The Astonishment here was much greater than at the Sight of my Scymiter. Hundreds fell down as if they had been struck dead; and even the Emperor, although he stood his Ground, could not recover himself in some time. I delivered up both my Pistols in the same Manner as I had done my Scymiter, and then my Pouch of Powder and Bullets; begging him that the former might be kept from Fire; for it would kindle with the smallest Spark, and blow up his Imperial Palace into the Air. I likewise delivered up my Watch, which the Emperor was very curious to see; and commanded two of his tallest Yeomen of the Guards to bear it on a Pole upon their Shoulders, as Dray-men in *England* do a Barrel of Ale. He was amazed at the continual Noise it made, and the Motion of the Minute-hand, which he could easily discern; for their Sight is much more acute than ours: I then gave up my Silver and Copper Money, my Purse with nine large Pieces of Gold, and some smaller ones; my Knife and Razor, my Comb and Silver Snuff-Box, my Handkerchief and Journal Book. My Scymiter, Pistols, and Pouch, were conveyed in Carriages to his Majesty's Stores; but the rest of my Goods were returned me.

I had, as I before observed, one private Pocket which escaped their Search, wherein there was a Pair of Spectacles (which I sometimes use for the Weakness of my Eyes) a Pocket Perspective, and several other little Conveniences; which being of no Consequence to the Emperor, I did not think my self bound in Honour to discover; and I apprehended they might be lost or spoiled if I ventured them out of my Possession.

CHAPTER THREE

THE AUTHOR DIVERTS THE EMPEROR AND HIS NOBILITY OF BOTH
SEXES, IN A VERY UNCOMMON MANNER. THE DIVERSIONS OF THE
COURT OF LILLIPUT DESCRIBED. THE AUTHOR HATH HIS LIBERTY
GRANTED HIM UPON CERTAIN CONDITIONS.

MY Gentleness and good Behaviour had gained so far on the Emperor and his Court, and indeed upon the Army and People in general, that I began to conceive Hopes of getting my Liberty in a short Time. The Natives came by Degrees to be less apprehensive of any Danger from me. I would sometimes lie down, and let five or six of them dance on my Hand. And at last the Boys and Girls would venture to come and play at Hide and Seek in my Hair. I had now made a good Progress in understanding and speaking their Language. The Emperor had a mind one Day to entertain me with several of the Country Shows; wherein they exceed all Nations I have known, both for Dexterity and Magnificence. I was diverted with none so much as that of the Rope-Dancers, performed upon a slender white Thread, extended about two Foot, and twelve Inches from the Ground.

This Diversion is only practised by those Persons, who are Candidates for great Employments, and high Favour, at Court. They are trained in this Art from their Youth, and are not always of noble Birth, or liberal Education. When a great Office is vacant, either by Death of Disgrace, (which often happens) five or six of those Candidates petition the Emperor to entertain his Majesty and the Court with a Dance on the Rope; and whoever jumps the highest without falling, succeeds in the Office. Very often the chief Ministers themselves are commanded to shew their Skill, and to convince the Emperor that they have not lost their Faculty. *Flimnap*, the Treasurer, is allowed to cut a Caper on the strait Rope, at least an Inch higher than any other Lord in the whole Empire. I have seen him do the Summer-set several times together, upon a Trencher fixed on the rope, which is no thicker than a common Pack-thread in *England*. My Friend *Reldresal*, principal Secretary for private Affairs, is, in my Opinion, if I am not partial, the second after the Treasurer.

These Diversions are often attended with fatal Accidents, whereof great Numbers are on Record. I my self have seen two or three Candidates break a Limb. But the Danger is much greater, when the Ministers themselves are commanded to shew their Dexterity: For, by contending to excel themselves and their Fellows, they strain so far, that there is hardly one of them who hath not received a Fall; and some of them two or three. I was assured, that a Year or two before my Arrival, *Flimnap* would have infallibly broke his Neck, if one of the *King's Cushions*, that accidentally lay on the Ground, had not weakened the Force of his Fall.

There is likewise another Diversion, which is only shewn before the Emperor and Empress, and first Minister, upon particular Occasions. The Emperor lays on a Table three fine silken Threads of six Inches long. One is Blue, the other Red, and the third Green. These Threads are proposed as Prizes, for those Persons whom the Emperor hath a mind to distinguish by a peculiar Mark of his Favour. The Ceremony is performed in his Majesty's great Chamber of State; where the Candidates are to undergo a Tryal of Dexterity very different from the former; and such as I have not observed the least Resemblance of in any other Country of the old or the new World. The Emperor holds a Stick in his Hands, both Ends parallel to the Horizon, while the Candidates advancing one by one, some-times leap over the Stick, sometimes creep under it backwards and forwards several times, according as the Stick is advanced or depressed. Sometimes the Emperor holds one End of the Stick, and his first Minister the other; sometimes the Minister has it entirely to himself. Whoever performs his Part with most Agility, and holds out the longest in *leaping* and *creeping*, is rewarded with the Blue-coloured Silk; the Red is given to the next, and the Green to the third, which they all wear girt twice round about the Middle; and you see few great Persons about this Court, who are not adorned with one of these Girdles.

The Horses of the Army, and those of the Royal Stables, having been daily led before me, were no longer shy, but would come up to my very Feet, without starting. The Riders would leap them over my Hand as I held it on the Ground; and one of the Emperor's Huntsmen, upon a large Courser, took my Foot, Shoe and all; which was indeed a prodigious Leap. I had the good Fortune to divert the Emperor one Day, after a very extraordinary Manner. I desired he would order several Sticks of two Foot high, and the Thickness of an ordinary Cane, to be brought me; whereupon his Majesty commanded the Master of his Woods to give Directions accordingly; and the next Morning six Wood-men arrived with as many Carriages, drawn by eight Horses to each. I took nine of these Sticks, and fixing them firmly in the Ground in a Quadrangular Figure, two Foot and a half square; I took four other Sticks, and tyed them parallel at each Corner, about two Foot from the Ground; and then I fastened my Handkerchief to the nine Sticks that stood erect; and extended it on all Sides, till it was as tight as the Top of a Drum; and the four parallel Sticks rising about five Inches higher than the Handkerchief, served as Ledges on each Side. When I had finished my Work, I desired the Emperor to let a Troop of his best Horse, Twenty-four in Number, come and exercise upon this Plain. His Majesty approved of the Proposal, and I took them up one by one in my Hands, ready mounted and armed, with the proper Officers to exercise them. As soon as they got into Order, they divided into two Parties, performed mock Skirmishes, discharged blunt Arrows, drew their Swords, fled and pursued, attacked and retired; and in short discovered the best military Discipline I ever beheld. The Emperor was so much delighted, that he ordered this Entertainment to be repeated several Days; and once was pleased to be lifted up, and give the Word of Command; and, with great Difficulty, persuaded even the Empress her self to let me hold her in her close Chair, within two Yards of the Stage, from whence she was able to take a full View of the whole Performance. It was my good Fortune that no ill Accident happened in these Entertainments; only once a fiery Horse that belonged to one of the Captains, pawing with his Hoof struck a Hole in my

Handkerchief, and his Foot slipping, he over-threw his Rider and himself; but I immediately relieved them both: For covering the Hole with one Hand, I set down the Troop with the other, in the same Manner as I took them up. The Horse that fell was strained in the left Shoulder, but the Rider got no Hurt, and I repaired my Handkerchief as well as I could: However, I would not trust to the Strength of it any more in such dangerous Enterprizes.

About two or three Days before I was set at Liberty, as I was entertaining the Court with these Kinds of Feats, there arrived an Express to inform his Majesty, that some of his Subjects riding near the Place where I was first taken up, had seen a great black Substance lying on the Ground, very oddly shaped, extending its Edges round as wide as his Majesty's Bedchamber, and rising up in the Middle as high as a Man. That it was no living Creature, as they at first apprehended; for it lay on the Grass without Motion, and some of them had walked round it several Times: That by mounting upon each others Shoulders, they had got to the Top, which was flat and even; and stamping upon it, they found it was hollow within: That they humbly conceived it might be something belonging to the *Man-Mountain*; and if his Majesty pleased, they would undertake to bring it with only five Horses. I presently knew what they meant; and was glad at Heart to receive this Intelligence. It seems, upon my first reaching the Shore, after our Shipwreck, I was in such Confusion, that before I came to the Place where I went to sleep, my Hat, which I had fastened with a String to my Head while I was rowing, and had stuck on all the Time I was swimming, fell off after I came to Land; the String, as I conjecture, breaking by some Accident which I never observed, but thought my Hat had been lost at Sea. I intreated his Imperial Majesty to give Orders it might be brought to me as soon as possible, describing to him the Use and the Nature of it: And the next Day the Waggoners arrived with it, but not in a very good Condition; they had bored two Holes in the Brim, within an Inch and a half of the Edge, and fastened two Hooks in the Holes; these Hooks were tyed by a long Cord to the Harness, and thus my Hat was dragged along for above half an *English* Mile: but the Ground in that Country being extremely smooth and level, it received less Damage than I expected.

Two Days after this Adventure, the Emperor having ordered that Part of his Army, which quarters in and about his Metropolis, to be in a Readiness, took a fancy of diverting himself in a very singular Manner. He desired I would stand like a *Colossus*, with my Legs as far asunder as I conveniently could. He then commanded his General (who was an old experienced Leader, and a great Patron of mine) to draw up the Troops in close Order, and march them under me ; the Foot by Twenty-four in a Breast, and the Horse by Sixteen, with Drums beating, Colours flying, and Pikes advanced. This Body consisted of three Thousand Foot, and a Thousand Horse.

I had sent so many Memorials and Petitions for my Liberty, that his Majesty at length mentioned the Matter first in the Cabinet, and then in a full Council ; where it was opposed by none, except *Skyresh Bolgolam*, who was pleased, without any Provocation, to be my mortal Enemy. But it was carried against him by the whole Board, and confirmed by the Emperor. That Minister was *Galbet*, or Admiral of the Realm ; very much in his Master's Confidence, and a Person well versed in Affairs, but of a morose and sour Complection. However, he was at length persuaded to comply ; but prevailed that the Articles and Conditions upon which I should be set free, and to which I must swear, should be drawn up by himself. These Articles were brought to me by *Skyresh Bolgolam* in Person, attended by two under Secretaries, and several Persons of Distinction. I have made a Translation of the whole Instrument, Word for Word, as near as I was able ; which I here offer to the Publick.

GOLBASTO MOMAREN EVLAME GURDILO SHEFIN MULLY ULLY GUE, most Mighty Emperor of *Lilliput*, Delight and Terror of the Universe, whose Dominions extend five Thousand Blustrugs, (about twelve Miles in Circumference) to the Extremities of the Globe : Monarch of all Monarchs : Taller than the Sons of Men ; whose Feet press down to the Center, and whose Head strikes against the Sun : At whose Nod the Princes of the Earth shake their Knees ; pleasant as the Spring, comfortable as the Summer, fruitful as Autumn, dreadful as Winter.

His most sublime Majesty proposeth to the *Man-Mountain*, lately arrived at our Celestial Dominions, the following Articles, which by a solemn Oath he shall be obliged to perform.

First, The *Man-Mountain* shall not depart from our Dominions, without our Licence under our Great Seal.

Secondly, He shall not presume to come into our Metropolis, without our express Order; at which time, the Inhabitants shall have two Hours Warning, to keep within their Doors.

Thirdly, The said *Man-Mountain* shall confine his Walks to our principal high Roads; and not offer to walk or lie down in a Meadow, or Field of Corn.

Fourthly, As he walks the said Roads, he shall take the utmost Care not to trample upon the Bodies of any of our loving Subjects, their Horses, or Carriages; nor take any of our said Subjects into his Hands, without their own Consent.

Fifthly, If an Express require extraordinary Dispatch; the *Man-Mountain* shall be obliged to carry in his Pocket the Messenger and Horse, a six Days Journey once in every Moon, and return the said Messenger back (if so required) safe to our Imperial Presence.

Sixthly, He shall be our Ally against our Enemies in the Island of *Blefuscu*, and do his utmost to destroy their Fleet, which is now preparing to invade Us.

Seventhly, That the said *Man-Mountain* shall, at his Times of Leisure, be aiding and assisting to our Workmen, in helping to raise certain great Stones, towards covering the Wall of the principal Park, and other our Royal Buildings.

Eighthly, That the said *Man-Mountain* shall, in two Moons Time, deliver in an exact survey of the Circumference of our Dominions, by a Computation of his own Paces round the Coast.

Lastly, That upon his solemn Oath to observe all the above Articles, the said *Man-Mountain* shall have a daily Allowance of Meat and Drink, sufficient for the Support of 1728 of our Subjects; with free Access to our Royal Person, and other Marks of our Favour. Given at our Palace at *Belfaborac* the Twelfth Day of the Ninety-first Moon of our Reign.

I swore and subscribed to these Articles with great Chearfulness and Content, although some of them were not so honourable as I could have wished; which proceeded wholly from the Malice of *Skyresh Bolgolam* the High Admiral: Whereupon my Chains were immediately unlocked, and I was at full Liberty: The Emperor himself, in Person, did me the Honour to be by at the whole Ceremony. I made my Acknowledgments, by prostrating myself at his Majesty's Feet: But he commanded me to rise; and after many gracious Expressions, which, to avoid the Censure of Vanity, I shall not repeat; he added, that he hoped I should prove a useful Servant, and well deserve all the Favours he had already conferred upon me, or might do for the future.

CHAPTER FOUR

MILDENDO, THE METROPOLIS OF LILLIPUT, DESCRIBED, TOGETHER WITH THE EMPEROR'S PALACE. A CONVERSATION BETWEEN THE AUTHOR AND A PRINCIPAL SECRETARY, CONCERNING THE AFFAIRS OF THAT EMPIRE. THE AUTHOR'S OFFERS TO SERVE THE EMPEROR IN HIS WARS.

THE first Request I made after I had obtained my Liberty, was, that I might have Licence to see *Mildendo*, the Metropolis; which the Emperor easily granted me, but with a special Charge to do no Hurt, either to the Inhabitants, or their Houses. The People had Notice by Proclamation of my Design to visit the Town. The Wall which encompassed it, is two Foot and an half high, and at least eleven Inches broad, so that a Coach and Horses may be driven very safely round it;

and it is flanked with strong Towers at the Foot Distance. I
stept over the great *Western* Gate, and passed very gently, and
sideling through the two principal Streets, only in my short
Waistcoat, for fear of damaging the Roofs and Eves of the
Houses with the Skirts of my Coat. I walked with the
utmost Circumspection, to avoid treading on any Stragglers,
who might remain in the Streets, although the Orders were
very strict, that all People should keep in their Houses,
at their own Peril. The Garret Windows and Tops of Houses
were so crowded with Spectators, that I thought in all my
Travels I had not seen a more populous Place. The City is
an exact Square, each Side of the Wall being five Hundred
Foot long. The two great Streets which run cross and divide
it into four Quarters, are five Foot wide. The Lanes and Alleys
which I could not enter, but only viewed them as I passed, are
from Twelve to Eighteen Inches. The Town is capable of
holding five Hundred Thousand Souls. The Houses are from
three to five Stories. The Shops and Markets are well provided.

The Emperor's Palace is in the Center of the City, where
the two great Streets meet. It is inclosed by a Wall of two
Foot high, and Twenty Foot distant from the Buildings. I had
his Majesty's Permission to step over this Wall; and the Space
being so wide between that and the Palace, I could easily view
it on every Side. The outward Court is a Square of Forty Foot,
and includes two other Courts: In the inmost are the Royal
Apartments, which I was very desirous to see, but found it
extremely difficult; for the great Gates, from one Square into
another, were but Eighteen Inches high, and seven Inches
wide. Now the Buildings of the outer Court were at least five
Foot high; and it was impossible for me to stride over them,
without infinite Damage to the Pile, although the Walls were
strongly built of hewn Stone, and four Inches thick. At the
same time, the Emperor had a great Desire that I should see
the Magnificence of his Palace: But this I was not able to do
till three Days after, which I spent in cutting down with my
Knife some of the largest Trees in the Royal Park, about an
Hundred Yards distant from the City. Of these Trees I made
two Stools, each about three Foot high, and strong enough to
bear my Weight. The People having received Notice a second

time, I went again through the City to the Palace, with my two Stools in my Hands. When I came to the Side of the outer Court, I stood upon one Stool, and took the other in my Hand: This I lifted over the Roof, and gently set it down on the Space between the first and second Court, which was eight Foot wide. I then stept over the Buildings very conveniently from one Stool to the other, and drew up the first after me with a hooked Stick. By this Contrivance I got into the inmost Court; and lying down upon my Side, I applied my Face to the Windows of the middle Stories, which were left open on Purpose, and discovered the most splendid Apartments that can be imagined. There I saw the Empress and the young Princes in their several Lodgings, with their chief Attendants about them. Her Imperial Majesty was pleased to smile very graciously upon me and gave me out of the Window her Hand to kiss.

One Morning, about a Fortnight after I had obtained my Liberty, *Reldresal*, Principal Secretary (as they style him) of private Affairs, came to my House, attended only by one Servant. He ordered his Coach to wait at a Distance, and desired I would give him an Hour's Audience; which I readily consented to, on Account of his Quality, and Personal Merits, as well as of the many good Offices he had done me during my Sollicitations at Court. I offered to lie down, that he might the more conveniently reach my Ear; but he chose rather to let me hold him in my Hand during our Conversation. He began with Compliments on my Liberty; said, he might pretend to some Merit in it; but, however, added, that if it had not been for the present Situation of things at Court, perhaps I might not have obtained it so soon. For, *said he*, as flourishing a Condition as we appear to be in to Foreigners, we labour under two mighty Evils; a violent Faction at home, and the Danger of an Invasion by a most potent Enemy from abroad. As to the first, you are to understand, that for above seventy Moons past, there have been two struggling Parties in this Empire, under the Names of *Tramecksan*, and *Slamecksan*, from the high and low Heels on their Shoes, by which they distinguish themselves.

It is alleged indeed, that the high Heels are most agreeable to our ancient Constitution: But however this be, his Majesty hath determined to make use of only low Heels in the Administration of the Government, and all Offices in the Gift of the Crown; as you cannot but observe; and particularly, that his Majesty's Imperial Heels are lower at least by a *Drurr* than any of his Court; (*Drurr* is a Measure about the fourteenth Part of an Inch.) The Animosities between these two Parties run so high, that they will neither eat nor drink, nor talk with each other. We compute the *Tramecksan*, or High-Heels, to exceed us in Number; but the Power is wholly on our Side. We apprehend his Imperial Highness, the Heir to the Crown, to have some Tendency towards the High-Heels; at least we can plainly discover one of his Heels higher than the other; which gives him a Hobble in his Gait. Now, in the midst of these intestine Disquiets, we are threatened with an Invasion from the Island of *Blefuscu*, which is the other great Empire of the Universe, almost as large and powerful as this of his Majesty. For as to what we have heard you affirm, that there are other Kingdoms and States in the World, inhabited by human Creatures as large as your self, our Philosophers are in much Doubt; and would rather conjecture that you dropt from the Moon, or one of the Stars; because it is certain, that an hundred Mortals of your Bulk, would, in a short Time, destroy all the Fruits and Cattle of his Majesty's Dominions. Besides, our Histories of six Thousand Moons make no mention of any other Regions, than the two great Empires of *Lilliput* and *Blefuscu*. Which two mighty Powers have, as I was going to tell you, been engaged in a most obstinate War for six and thirty Moons past. It began upon the following Occasion. It is allowed on all Hands, that the Primitive Way of breaking Eggs before we eat them, was upon the larger End: But his present Majesty's Grand-father, while he was a Boy, going to eat an Egg, and breaking it according to the ancient Practice, happened to cut one of his Fingers. Whereupon the Emperor his Father, published an Edict, commanding all his Subjects, upon great Penalties, to break the smaller End of their Eggs. The People so highly resented this Law, that our Histories tell us, there have been six Rebellions raised on that Account; wherein one Emperor lost his Life, and another his Crown. These civil Commotions were constantly fomented by the

Monarchs of *Blefuscu*; and when they were quelled, the Exiles always fled for Refuge to that Empire. It is computed, that eleven Thousand Persons have, at several Times, suffered Death, rather than submit to break their Eggs at the smaller End. Many hundred large Volumes have been published upon this Controversy: But the Books of the *Big-Endians* have been long forbidden, and the whole Party rendered incapable by Law of holding Employments. Now the *Big-Endian* Exiles have found so much Credit in the Emperor of *Blefuscu's* Court; and so much private Assistance and Encouragement from their Party here at home, that a bloody War hath been carried on between the two Empires for six and thirty Moons with various Success; during which Time we have lost Forty Capital Ships, and a much greater Number of smaller Vessels, together with thirty thousand of our best Seamen and Soldiers; and the Damage received by the Enemy is reckoned to be somewhat greater than ours. However, they have now equipped a numerous Fleet, and are just preparing to make a Descent upon us: And his Imperial Majesty, placing great Confidence in your Valour and Strength, hath commanded me to lay this Account of his affairs before you.

I desired the Secretary to present my humble Duty to the Emperor, and to let him know, that I thought it would not become me, who was a Foreigner, to interfere with Parties; but I was ready, with the Hazard of my Life, to defend his Person and State against all Invaders.

CHAPTER FIVE

THE AUTHOR BY AN EXTRAORDINARY STRATAGEM PREVENTS AN
INVASION. A HIGH TITLE OF HONOUR IS CONFERRED UPON HIM.
AMBASSADORS ARRIVE FROM THE EMPEROR OF BLEFUSCU, AND SUE
FOR PEACE.

THE Empire of *Blefuscu*, is an Island situated to the North
North-East Side of *Lilliput*, from whence it is parted only
by a Channel of eight Hundred Yards wide. I had not yet seen
it, and upon this Notice of an intended Invasion, I avoided
appearing on that Side of the Coast, for fear of being discovered
by some of the Enemie's Ships who had received no Intelligence
of me; all intercourse between the two Empires having been
strictly forbidden during the War, upon Pain of Death; and
an Embargo laid by our Emperor upon all Vessels whatsoever.
I communicated to his Majesty a Project I had formed of seizing
the Enemie's whole Fleet; which, as our Scouts assured us,
lay at Anchor in the Harbour ready to sail with the first fair
Wind. I consulted the more experienced Seamen, upon the
Depth of the Channel, which they had often plummed; who
told me, that in the Middle at high Water it was seventy
Glumgluffs deep, which is about six Foot of *European* Measure;
and the rest of it fifty *Glumgluffs* at most. I walked to the
North-East Coast over against *Blefuscu*; where, lying down
behind a Hillock, I took out my small Pocket Perspective Glass,
and viewed the Enemy's Fleet at Anchor, consisting of about
fifty Men of War, and a great Number of Transports: I then
came back to my House, and gave Order (for which I had a
Warrant) for a great Quantity of the strongest Cable and Bars
of Iron. The Cable was about as thick as Packthread, and the
Bars of the Length and Size of a Knitting-Needle. I trebled
the Cable to make it stronger; and for the same Reason I
twisted three of the Iron Bars together, binding the Extremities
into a Hook. Having thus fixed fifty Hooks to as many Cables,
I went back to the North-East Coast, and putting off my Coat,

Shoes, and Stockings, walked into the Sea in my Leathern Jerken, about half an Hour before high Water. I waded with what Haste I could, and swam in the Middle about thirty Yards until I felt the Ground; I arrived at the Fleet in less than half an Hour. The Enemy was so frighted when they saw me, that they leaped out of their Ships, and swam to Shore; where there could not be fewer than thirty thousand Souls. I then took my Tackling, and fastning a Hook to the Hole at the Prow of each, I tyed all the Cords together at the End. While I was thus employed, the Enemy discharged several Thousand Arrows, many of which stuck in my Hands and Face; and besides the excessive Smart, gave me much Disturbance in my Work. My greatest Apprehension was for my Eyes, which I should have infallibly lost, if I had not suddenly thought of an Expedient. I kept, among other little Necessaries, a Pair of Spectacles in a private Pocket, which, as I observed before, had escaped the Emperor's Searchers. These I took out, and fastened as strongly as I could upon my Nose; and thus armed went on boldly with my Work in spight of the Enemy's Arrows; many of which struck against the Glasses of my Spectacles, but without any other Effect, further than a little to discompose them. I had now fastened all the Hooks, and taking the Knot in my Hand, began to pull; but not a Ship would stir, for they were all too fast held by their Anchors; so that the boldest Part of my Enterprize remained. I therefore let go the Cord, and leaving the Hooks fixed to the Ships, I resolutely cut with my Knife the Cables that fastened the Anchors; receiving above two hundred Shots in my Face and Hands: Then I took up the knotted End of the Cables to which my Hooks were tyed; and with great Ease drew fifty of the Enemy's largest Men of War after me.

The *Blefuscudians*, who had not the least Imagination of what I intended were at first confounded with Astonishment. They had seen me cut the Cables, and thought my Design was only to let the Ships run a-drift, or fall foul on each other: But when they perceived the whole Fleet moving in Order, and saw me pulling at the End; they set up such a Scream of Grief and Dispair, that it is almost impossible to describe or conceive. When I had got out of Danger, I stopt a while to pick

out the Arrows that stuck in my Hands and Face, and rubbed
on some of the same Ointment that was given me at my first
Arrival, as I have formerly mentioned. I then took off my
Spectacles, and waiting about an Hour until the Tyde was a
little fallen, I waded through the Middle with my Cargo, and
arrived safe at the Royal Port of *Lilliput*.

The Emperor and his whole Court stood on the Shore,
expecting the Issue of this great Adventure. They saw the
Ships move forward in a large Half-Moon, but could not
discern me, who was up to my Breast in Water. When I
advanced to the Middle of the Channel, they were yet more in
Pain because I was under Water to my Neck. The Emperor
concluded me to be drowned, and that the Enemy's Fleet was
approaching in a hostile Manner : But he was soon eased of
of his Fears ; for the Channel growing shallower every Step
I made, I came in a short Time within Hearing ; and holding
up the End of the Cable by which the Fleet was fastened, I
cryed in a loud Voice. *Long live the most puissant Emperor of
Lilliput !* This great Prince received me at my Landing with
all possible Encomiums, and created me a *Nardac* upon the
Spot, which is the highest Title of Honour among them.

His Majesty desired I would take some other Opportunity
of bringing all the rest of his Enemy's Ships into his Ports.
And so unmeasurable is the Ambition of Princes, that he seemed
to think of nothing less than reducing the whole Empire of
Blefuscu into a Province, and governing it by a Viceroy ; of
destroying the *Big-Endian* Exiles, and compelling that People
to break the smaller End of their Eggs ; by which he would
remain sole Monarch of the whole World. But I endeavoured
to divert him from this Design. And I plainly protested, that I
would never be an Instrument of bringing a free and brave
People into Slavery : And when the Matter was debated in
Council, the wisest Part of the Ministry were of my Opinion.

This open bold Declaration of mine was so opposite to the
Schemes and Politicks of his Imperial Majesty, that he could
never forgive me : He mentioned it in a very artful Manner at
Council, where, I was told, that some of the wisest appeared,
at least by their Silence, to be of my Opinion ; but others, who
were my secret Enemies, could not forbear some Expressions,

which by a Side-wind reflected on me. And from this Time began an Intrigue between his Majesty, and a Junta of Ministers maliciously bent against me, which broke out in less than two Months, and had like to have ended in my utter Destruction.

About three Weeks after this Exploit, there arrived a solemn Embassy from *Blefuscu*, with humble Offers of a Peace ; which was soon concluded upon Conditions very advantageous to our Emperor; There were six Ambassadors, with a Train of about five Hundred Persons ; and their Entry was very magnificent, suitable to the Grandeur of their Master, and the Importance of their Business. When their Treaty was finished, wherein I did them several good Offices by the Credit I now had, or at least appeared to have at Court; their Excellencies, who were privately told how much I had been their Friend, made me a Visit in Form. They began with many Compliments upon my Valour and Generosity ; invited me to that Kingdom in the Emperor their Master's Name, and desired me to shew them some Proofs of my prodigious Strength.

When I had for some time entertained their Excellencies to their infinite Satisfaction and Surprize, I desired they would do me the Honour to present my most humble Respects to the Emperor their Master, the Renown of whose Virtues had so justly filled the whole World with Admiration, and whose Royal Person I resolved to attend before I returned to my own Country. Accordingly, the next time I had the Honour to see our Emperor, I desired his general Licence to wait on the *Blefuscudian* Monarch, which he was pleased to grant me, as I could plainly perceive, in a very cold Manner ; but could not guess the Reason, till I had a Whisper from a certain Person, that *Flimnap* and *Bolgolam* had represented my Intercourse with those Ambassadors, as a Mark of Disaffection, from which I am sure my Heart was wholly free.

CHAPTER SIX

OF THE INHABITANTS OF LILLIPUT; THEIR LAWS AND CUSTOMS.
THE AUTHOR'S WAY OF LIVING IN THAT COUNTRY.

ALTHOUGH I intend to leave the Description of this Empire
to a particular Treatise, yet in the mean time I am content
to gratify the curious Reader with some general Ideas. As the
common Size of the Natives is somewhat under Six Inches, so
there is an exact Proportion in all other Animals, as well as
Plants and Trees: For Instance, the tallest Horses and Oxen
are between four and five Inches in Height, the Sheep an Inch
and a half, more or less; their Geese about the Bigness of
a Sparrow; and so the several Gradations downwards, till you
come to the smallest, which, to my Sight, were almost invisible;
but Nature hath adapted the Eyes of the *Lilliputians* to all
Objects proper for their View: They see with great Exactness,
but at no great Distance. And to show the Sharpness of their
Sight towards Objects that are near, I have been much pleased
with observing a Cook pulling a Lark, which was not so large
as a common Fly; and a young Girl threading an invisible
Needle with invisible Silk. Their tallest Trees are about seven
Foot high; I mean some of those in the great Royal Park, the
Tops whereof I could but just reach with my Fist clinched.
The other Vegetables are in the same Proportion:

Their Manner of Writing is very peculiar; being neither
from the Left to the Right, like the *Europeans*; nor from the
Right to the Left, like the *Arabians*; nor from up to down, like
the *Chinese*; nor from down to up, like the *Cascagians*; but
aslant from one Corner of the Paper to the other, like Ladies
in *England*.

They bury their Dead with their Heads directly downwards;
because they hold an Opinion, that in eleven Thousand Moons
they are all to rise again; in which Period, the Earth (which
they conceive to be flat) will turn upside down, and by this
Means they shall, at their Resurrection, be found ready standing

on their Feet. The Learned among them confess the Absurdity of this Doctrine; but the practice still continues, in Compliance to the Vulgar.

There are some Laws and Customs in this Empire very peculiar; and if they were not so directly contrary to those of my own dear Country, I should be tempted to say a little in their Justification. It is only to be wished, that they were as well executed. The first I shall mention, relateth to Informers. All Crimes against the State, are punished here with the utmost Severity; but if the Person accused make his Innocence plainly to appear upon his Tryal, the Accuser is immediately put to an ignominious Death; and out of his Goods or Lands, the innocent Person is quadruply recompensed for the Loss of his Time, for the Danger he underwent, for the Hardship of his Imprisonment, and for all the Charges he hath been at in making his Defence. Or, if that Fund be deficient, it is largely supplyed by the Crown. The Emperor doth also confer on him some publick Mark of his Favour; and Proclamation is made of his innocence through the whole City.

They look upon Fraud as a greater Crime than Theft, and therefore seldom fail to punish it with Death: For they alledge, that Care and Vigilance, with a very common Understanding, may preserve a Man's Goods from Thieves; but Honesty hath no Fence against superior Cunning: And since it is necessary that there should be a perpetual Intercourse of buying and selling, and dealing upon Credit; where Fraud is permitted or connived at, or hath no Law to punish it, the honest Dealer is always undone, and the Knave gets the Advantage. I remember when I was once interceeding with the King for a Criminal who had wronged his Master of a great Sum of Money, which he had received by Order, and ran away with; and happening to tell his Majesty, by way of Extenuation, that it was only a Breach of Trust; the Emperor thought it monstrous in me to offer, as a Defence, the greatest Aggravation of the Crime.

Although we usually call Reward and Punishment, the two Hinges upon which all Government turns; yet I could never observe this Maxim to be put in Practice by any Nation except that of *Lilliput*. Whoever can there bring sufficient Proof that he hath strictly observed the Laws of his Country for Seventy-three Moons, hath a Claim to certain Privileges, according to his Quality and Condition of Life, with a proportionable Sum of Money out of a Fund appropriated for that Use : He likewise acquires the Title of *Snilpall*, or *Legal*, which is added to his Name, but doth not descend to his Posterity. And these People thought it a prodigious Defect of Policy among us, when I told them that our Laws were enforced only by Penalties, without any Mention of Reward. It is upon this account that the Image of Justice, in their Courts of Judicature, is formed with six Eyes, two before, as many behind, and on each Side one, to signify Circumspection ; with a Bag of Gold open in her right Hand, and a Sword sheathed in her left, to shew she is more disposed to reward than to punish.

And here it may perhaps divert the curious Reader, to give some Account of my Domestick, and my Manner of living in this Country, during a residence of nine Months and thirteen Days. Having a Head mechanically turned, and being likewise forced by Necessity, I had made for myself a Table and Chair convenient enough, out of the largest Trees in the Royal Park. Two hundred Sempstresses were employed to make me Shirts, and Linnen for my Bed and Table, all of the strongest and coarsest kind they could get ; which, however, they were forced to quilt together in several Folds ; for the thickest was some Degrees finer than Lawn. Their Linnen is usually three Inches wide, and three Foot make a Piece. The Sempstresses took my Measure as I lay on the Ground, one standing at my Neck, and another at my Mid-Leg, with a strong Cord extended, that each held by the End, while the third measured the Length of the Cord with a Rule of an Inch long. Then they measured my right Thumb, and desired no more ; for by a mathematical Computation, that twice round the Thumb is once round the Wrist, and so on to the Neck and the Waist ; and by the Help of my old Shirt, which I displayed on the Ground before them for a Pattern they fitted me exactly. Three hundred Taylors were employed in the same Manner to make me Clothes ; but they had another Contrivance for taking my Measure. I kneeled down, and they raised a Ladder from the Ground to my Neck ; upon this Ladder one of them mounted, and let fall a Plum-Line from my Collar to the Floor, which just answered the Length of my Coat; but my Waist and Arms I measured myself. When my Cloaths were finished, which was done in my House, (for the largest of theirs would not have been able to hold them) they looked like the Patchwork made by the Ladies in *England*, only that mine were all of a Colour.

I had three hundred Cooks to dress my Victuals, in little convenient Huts built about my House, where they and their Families lived, and prepared me two Dishes a-piece. I took up twenty Waiters in my Hand, and placed them on the Table; an hundred more attended below on the Ground, some with Dishes of Meat, and some with Barrels of Wine, and other Liquors, slung on their Shoulders; all which the Waiters drew up as I wanted, in a very ingenious Manner, by certain Cords, as we draw the Bucket up a Well in *Europe*. A Dish of their Meat was a good Mouthful, and a Barrel of their Liquor a reasonable Draught. Their Mutton yields to ours, but their Beef is excellent. I have had a Sirloin so large, that I have been forced to make three Bits of it; but this is rare. My Servants were astonished to see me eat it Bones and all, as in our Country we do the Leg of a Lark. Their Geese and Turkeys I usually eat at a Mouthful, and I must confess they far exceed ours. Of their smaller Fowl I could take up twenty or thirty at the End of my Knife.

One day his Imperial Majesty being informed of my Way of living, desired that himself, and his Royal Consort, with the young Princes of the Blood of both Sexes, might have the Happiness (as he was pleased to call it) of dining with me. They came accordingly, and I placed them upon Chairs of State on my Table, just over against me, with their Guards about them. *Flimnap* the Lord High Treasurer attended there likewise, with his white Staff; and I observed he often looked on me with a sour Countenance, which I would not seem to regard, but eat more than usual, in Honour to my dear Country, as well as to fill the Court with Admiration. I have some private Reasons to believe, that this Visit from his Majesty gave *Flimnap* an Opportunity of doing me ill Offices to his Master. That Minister had always been my secret Enemy, although he outwardly caressed me more than was usual to the Moroseness of his Nature. He represented to the Emperor the low Condition of his Treasury; that he was forced to take up Money at great Discount; that I had cost his Majesty about a Million and a half of *Sprugs*, (their greatest Gold Coin, about the Bigness of a Spangle;) and upon the whole, that it would be adviseable in the Emperor to take the first fair Occasion of dismissing me.

CHAPTER SEVEN

THE AUTHOR BEING INFORMED OF A DESIGN TO ACCUSE HIM OF HIGH TREASON, MAKES HIS ESCAPE TO BLEFUSCU. HIS RECEPTION THERE.

BEFORE I proceed to give an Account of my leaving this Kingdom, it may be proper to inform the Reader of a private Intrigue which had been for two Months forming against me.

I had been hitherto all my Life a Stranger to Courts, for which I was unqualified by the Meanness of my Condition. I had indeed heard and read enough of the Dispositions of great Princes and Ministers; but never expected to have found such terrible Effects of them in so remote a Country, governed, as I thought, by very different Maxims from those in *Europe*.

When I was just preparing to pay my Attendance on the Emperor of *Blefuscu*; a considerable Person at Court (to whom I had been very serviceable at a time when he lay under the highest Displeasure of his Imperial Majesty) came to my House very privately at Night in a close Chair, and without sending his Name, desired Admittance: The Chair-men were dismissed; I put the Chair, with his Lordship in it, into my Coat-Pocket; and giving Orders to a trusty Servant to say I was indisposed and gone to sleep, I fastened the Door of my House, placed the Chair on the Table, according to my usual Custom, and sat down by it. After the common Salutations were over, observing his Lordship's Countenance full of Concern; and enquiring into the Reason, he desired I would

hear him with Patience, in a Matter that highly concerned my
Honour and my Life. His Speech was to the following Effect,
for I took Notes of it as soon as he left me.

You are to know, said he, that several Committees of Council
have been lately called in the most private Manner on your
Account : And it is but two Days since his Majesty came to a
full Resolution.

You are very sensible that *Skyris Bolgolam* (*Galbet*, or High
Admiral) hath been your mortal Enemy almost ever since your
Arrival. His original Reasons I know not ; but his Hatred is
much increased since your great Success against *Blefuscu*, by
which his Glory, as Admiral, is obscured. This Lord, in
Conjunction with *Flimnap* the High Treasurer, whose Enmity
against you is notorious ; *Limtoc* the General, *Lalcon* the
Chamberlain, and *Balmuff* the grand Justiciary, have prepared
Articles of Impeachment against you, for Treason, and other
capital Crimes.

In the several Debates upon this Impeachment, it must be
confessed that his Majesty gave many Marks of his great
Lenity ; often urging the Services you had done him, and
endeavouring to extenuate your Crimes. The Treasurer and
Admiral insisted that you should be put to the most painful
and ignominious Death, by setting Fire on your House at
Night ; and the General was to attend with Twenty Thousand
Men armed with poisoned Arrows, to shoot you on the Face
and Hands. Some of your Servants were to have private Orders
to strew a poisonous Juice on your Shirts and Sheets, which
would soon make you tear your own Flesh, and die in the
utmost Torture. The General came into the same Opinion ; so
that for a long time there was a Majority against you. But his
Majesty resolving, if possible, to spare your Life, at last brought
off the Chamberlain.

Upon this Incident, *Reldresal*, principal Secretary for private
Affairs, who always approved himself your true Friend, was
commanded by the Emperor to deliver his Opinion, which he
accordingly did ; and therein justified the good Thoughts you
have of him. He allowed your Crimes to be great ; but that
still there was room for Mercy, the most commendable Virtue

in a Prince, and for which his Majesty was so justly celebrated. He said, the Friendship between you and him was so well known to the World, that perhaps the most honourable Board might think him partial: However, in Obedience to the Command he had received, he would freely offer his Sentiments. That if his Majesty, in Consideration of your Services, and pursuant to his own merciful Disposition, would please to spare your Life, and only give order to put out both your Eyes; he humbly conceived, that by this Expedient, Justice might in some measure be satisfied, and all the World would applaud the *Lenity* of the Emperor, as well as the fair and generous Proceedings of those who have the Honour to be his Counsellors. That the Loss of your Eyes would be no Impediment to your bodily Strength, by which you might still be useful to his Majesty. That Blindness is an Addition to Courage, by concealing Dangers from us; that the Fear you had for your Eyes, was the greatest Difficulty in bringing over the Enemy's Fleet; and it would be sufficient for you to see by the Eyes of the Ministers, since the greatest Princes do no more.

This Proposal was received with the utmost Disapprobation by the whole Board. *Bolgolam*, the Admiral, could not preserve his Temper; but rising up in Fury, said, he wondered how the Secretary durst presume to give his Opinion for preserving the Life of a Traytor.

The Treasurer was of the same Opinion; he shewed to what Streights his Majesty's Revenue was reduced by the Charge of maintaining you, which would soon grow insupportable: That the Secretary's Expedient of putting out your Eyes, was so far from being a Remedy against this Evil, that it would probably increase it; as it is manifest from the common Practice of blinding some Kind of Fowl, after which they fed the faster, and grew sooner fat: That his sacred Majesty, and the Council, who are your Judges, were in their own Consciences fully convinced of your Guilt; which was a sufficient Argument to condemn you to death, without the *formal Proofs required by the strict Letter of the Law*.

But his Imperial Majesty fully determined against capital Punishment, was graciously pleased to say, that since the Council thought the Loss of your Eyes too easy a Censure, some other may be inflicted hereafter. And your Friend the Secretary humbly desiring to be heard again, in Answer to what the Treasurer had objected concerning the great Charge his Majesty was at in maintaining you; said, that his Excellency, who had the sole Disposal of the Emperor's Revenue, might easily provide against this Evil, by gradually lessening your Establishment; by which, for want of sufficient Food, you would grow weak and faint, and lose your Appetite, and consequently decay and consume in a few Months; neither would the Stench of your Carcass be then so dangerous, when it should become more than half diminished; and immediately upon your Death, five or six Thousand of his Majesty's Subjects might, in two or three Days, cut your Flesh from your Bones, take it away by Cart-loads, and bury it in distant Parts to prevent Infection; leaving the Skeleton as a Monument of Admiration to Posterity.

In three Days your Friend the Secretary will be directed to come to your House, and read before you the Articles of Impeachment; and then to signify the great *Lenity* and Favour of his Majesty and Council; whereby you are only condemned to the Loss of your Eyes, which his Majesty doth not question you will gratefully and humbly submit to; and Twenty of his Majesty's Surgeons will attend, in order to see the Operation well performed, by discharging very sharp pointed Arrows into the Balls of your Eyes, as you lie on the Ground.

I leave to your Prudence what Measures you will take; and to avoid Suspicion, I must immediately return in as private a Manner as I came.

His Lordship did so, and I remained alone, under many Doubts and Perplexities of Mind.

At last I fixed upon a Resolution, for which it is probable I may incur some Censure, and not unjustly; for I confess I owe the preserving of my Eyes, and consequently my Liberty, to my own great Rashness and Want of Experience: Because if I had then known the Nature of Princes and Ministers, which I have since observed in many other Courts, and their Methods of treating Criminals less obnoxious than myself; I should with great Alacrity and Readiness have submitted to so *easy* a Punishment. But hurried on by the Precipitancy of Youth;

and having his Imperial Majesty's Licence to pay my Attendance upon the Emperor of *Blefuscu* ; I took this Opportunity, before the three Days were elapsed, to send a Letter to my Friend the Secretary, signifying my Resolution of setting out that Morning for *Blefuscu,* pursuant to the Leave I had got ; and without waiting for an Answer, I went to that Side of the Island where our Fleet lay. I seized a large Man of War, tied a Cable to the Prow, and lifting up the Anchors, I stript myself, put my Cloaths (together with my Coverlet, which I carryed under my Arm) into the Vessel ; and drawing it after me, between wading and swimming, arrived at the Royal Port of *Blefuscu,* where the People had long expected me : They lent me two Guides to direct me to the Capital City, which is of the same Name ; I held them in my Hands until I came within two Hundred Yards of the Gate ; and desired them to signify my Arrival to one of the Secretaries, and let him know, I there waited his Majesty's Commands. I had an Answer in about an Hour, that his Majesty, attended by the Royal Family, and great Officers of the Court, was coming out to receive me. I advanced a Hundred Yards ; the Emperor, and his Train, alighted from their Horses, the Empress and Ladies from their Coaches ; and I did not perceive they were in any Fright or Concern. I lay on the Ground to kiss his Majesty's and the Empress's Hand. I told his Majesty, that I was come according to my Promise, and with the Licence of the Emperor my Master, to have the Honour of seeing so mighty a Monarch, and to offer him any Service in my Power, consistent with my Duty to my own Prince ; not mentioning a Word of my Disgrace, because I had hitherto no regular Information of it, and might suppose myself wholly ignorant of any such Design ; neither could I reasonably conceive that the Emperor would discover the Secret while I was out of his Power : Wherein, however, it soon appeared I was deceived.

I shall not trouble the Reader with the particular Account of my Reception at this Court, which was suitable to the Generosity of so great a Prince ; nor of the Difficulties I was in for want of a House and Bed, being forced to lie on the Ground, wrapt up in my Coverlet.

CHAPTER EIGHT

THE AUTHOR, BY A LUCKY ACCIDENT, FINDS MEANS TO LEAVE
BLEFUSCU ; AND, AFTER SOME DIFFICULTIES, RETURNS SAFE TO HIS
NATIVE COUNTRY.

THREE Days after my Arrival, walking out of Curiosity to
the North-East Coast of the Island ; I observed, about
half a League off, in the Sea, somewhat that looked like a Boat
overturned : I pulled off my Shoes and Stockings, and wading
two or three Hundred Yards, I found the Object to approach
nearer by Force of the Tide ; and then plainly saw it to be a
real Boat, which I supposed might, by some Tempest, have
been driven from a Ship. Whereupon I returned immediately
towards the City, and desired his Imperial Majesty to lend me
Twenty of the tallest Vessels he had left after the Loss of his
Fleet, and three Thousand Seamen under the Command of
his Vice-Admiral. This Fleet sailed round, while I went back
the shortest Way to the Coast where I first discovered the Boat ;
I found the Tide had driven it still nearer ; the Seamen were
all provided with Cordage, which I had beforehand twisted to
a sufficient Strength. When the Ships came up, I stript myself,
and waded till I came within an Hundred Yards of the Boat ;
after which I was forced to swim till I got up to it. The Seamen
threw me the End of the Cord, which I fastened to a Hole in
the fore-part of the Boat, and the other End to a Man of War :
But I found all my Labour to little Purpose ; for being out of
my Depth, I was not able to work. In this Necessity, I was
forced to swim behind, and push the Boat forwards as often as
I could, with one of my Hands ; and the Tide favouring me,
I advanced so far, that I could just hold up my Chin and feel
the Ground. I rested two or three Minutes, and then gave the
Boat another Shove, and so on till the Sea was no higher than
my Arm-pits. And now the most laborious Part being over,
I took out my other Cables which were stowed in one of the
Ships, and fastening them first to the Boat, and then to nine

of the Vessels which attended me; the Wind being favourable, the Seamen towed, and I shoved till we arrived within forty Yards of the Shore; and waiting till the Tide was out, I got dry to the Boat, and by the Assistance of two Thousand Men, with Ropes and Engines, I made a shift to turn it on its Bottom, and found it was but little damaged.

I shall not trouble the Reader with the Difficulties I was under by the Help of certain Paddles, which cost me ten Days making, to get my Boat to the Royal Port of *Blefuscu*; where a mighty Concourse of People appeared upon my Arrival, full of Wonder at the Sight of so prodigious a Vessel. I told the Emperor, that my good Fortune had thrown this Boat in my Way, to carry me to some Place from whence I might return into my native Country; and begged his Majesty's Orders for getting Materials to fit it up; together with his Licence to depart; which, after some kind Expostulations, he was pleased to grant.

In about a Month when all was prepared, I sent to receive his Majesty's Commands, and to take my leave. The Emperor and Royal Family came out of the Palace; I lay down on my Face to kiss his Hand, which he very graciously gave me; so did the Empress, and young Princes of the Blood. His Majesty presented me with fifty Purses of two hundred *Sprugs* a-piece, together with his Picture at full length, which I put immediately into one of my Gloves, to keep it from being hurt. The Ceremonies at my Departure were too many to trouble the Reader with at this time.

I stored the Boat with the Carcasses of an hundred Oxen, and three hundred Sheep, with Bread and Drink proportionable, and as much Meat ready dressed as four hundred Cooks could provide. I took with me six Cows and two Bulls alive, with as many Yews and Rams, intending to carry them into my own Country and propagate the Breed. And to feed them on board, I had a good Bundle of Hay, and a Bag of Corn. I would gladly have taken a Dozen of the Natives; but this was a thing the Emperor would by no Means permit; and besides a diligent Search into my Pockets, his Majesty engaged my Honour not to carry away any of his Subjects, although with their own Consent and Desire.

Having thus prepared all things as well as I was able; I set sail on the Twenty-fourth Day of *September* 1701, at six in the Morning; and when I had gone about four Leagues to the Northward, the Wind being at South-East; at six in the Evening, I descryed a small Island about half a League to the North West. I advanced forward, and cast Anchor on the Lee-side of the Island, which seemed to be uninhabited. I then took some Refreshment, and went to my Rest. I slept well, and as I conjecture at least six Hours; for I found the Day broke in two Hours after I awaked. It was a clear Night; I eat my Breakfast before the Sun was up; and heaving Anchor, the Wind being favourable, I steered the same Course that I had done the Day before, wherein I was directed by my Pocket-Compass. My Intention was to reach, if possible, one of those Islands, which I had reason to believe lay to the North-East of *Van Diemen's* Land. I discovered nothing all that Day; but upon the next, about three in the Afternoon, when I had by my Computation made Twenty-four Leagues from *Blefuscu*, I descryed a Sail steering to the South-East; my Course was due East. I hailed her, but could get no Answer; yet I found I gained upon her, for the Wind slackened. I made all the Sail I could, and in half an Hour she spyed me, then hung out her Antient, and discharged a Gun. It is not easy to express the Joy I was in upon the unexpected Hope of once more seeing my beloved Country, and the dear Pledges I had left in it. The Ship slackened her Sails, and I came up with her between five and six in the Evening, *September* 26; but my Heart leapt within me to see her *English* Colours. I put my Cows and Sheep into my Coat-Pockets, and got on board with all my Cargo of Provisions. The Vessel was an *English* Merchant-man, returning from *Japan* by the *North* and *South Seas*; the Captain, Mr. *John Biddel* of *Deptford*, a very civil Man, and an excellent Sailor. We were now in the Latitude of 30 Degrees South; there were about fifty Men in the Ship; and here I met an old Comrade of mine, one *Peter Williams*, who gave me a good Character to the Captain. This Gentleman treated me with Kindness and desired I would let him know what Place I came from last, and whither I was bound; which I did in few Words; but he thought I was raving, and that the Dangers I underwent had disturbed my Head; whereupon I took my black Cattle and Sheep out of my Pocket, which, after great Astonishment, clearly convinced him of my Veracity. I then shewed him the Gold given me by the Emperor of *Blefuscu*, together with his Majesty's Picture at full Length, and some other Rarities of that Country. I gave him two Purses of two Hundred *Sprugs* each, and promised, when we arrived in *England*, to make him a Present of a Cow and a Sheep big with Young.

We arrived in the *Downs* on the 13th of *April* 1702. I had only one Misfortune, that the Rats on board carried away one of my Sheep; I found her Bones in a Hole, picked clean from the Flesh. The rest of my Cattle I got safe on Shore, and set them a grazing in a Bowling-green at *Greenwich*, where the Fineness of the Grass made them feed very heartily, although I had always feared the contrary : Neither could I possibly have preserved them in so long a Voyage, if the Captain had not allowed me some of his best Bisket, which rubbed to Powder, and mingled with Water, was their constant Food. The short Time I continued in *England*, I made a considerable Profit by shewing my Cattle to many Persons of Quality, and others : And before I began my second Voyage, I sold them for six Hundred Pounds. Since my last Return, I find the Breed is considerably increased, especially the Sheep ; which I hope will prove much to the Advantage of the Woollen Manufacture, by the Fineness of the Fleeces.

I stayed but two Months with my Wife and Family ; for my insatiable Desire of seeing foreign Countries would suffer me to continue no longer. I left fifteen Hundred Pounds with my Wife, and fixed her in a good House at *Redriff*. My remaining Stock I carried with me, Part in Money, and Part in Goods, in Hopes to improve my Fortunes. My eldest Uncle, *John*, had left me an Estate in Land, near *Epping*, of about Thirty Pounds a Year ; and I had a long Lease of the *Black-Bull* in *Fetter-Lane*, which yielded me as much more : So that I was not in any Danger of leaving my Family upon the Parish. My Son *Johnny*, named so after his Uncle, was at the Grammar School, and a towardly Child. My Daughter *Betty* (who is now well married, and has Children) was then at her Needle-Work. I took Leave of my Wife, and Boy and Girl, with Tears on both Sides ; and went on board the *Adventure*, a Merchant-Ship of three Hundred Tons, bound for *Surat*, Captain *John Nicholas* of *Liverpool*, Commander. But my Account of this Voyage must be referred to the second Part of my Travels.

PART TWO

A VOYAGE TO BROBDINGNAG

CHAPTER ONE

A GREAT STORM DESCRIBED. THE LONG BOAT SENT TO FETCH
WATER, THE AUTHOR GOES WITH IT TO DISCOVER THE COUNTRY.
HE IS LEFT ON SHOAR, IS SEIZED BY ONE OF THE NATIVES, AND
CARRIED TO A FARMER'S HOUSE. HIS RECEPTION THERE, WITH
SEVERAL ACCIDENTS THAT HAPPENED THERE. A DESCRIPTION OF
THE INHABITANTS.

HAVING been condemned by Nature and Fortune to an
active and restless Life; in two Months after my Return,
I again left my Native Country, and took Shipping in the
Downs on the 20th Day of *June* 1702, in the *Adventure*, Capt.
John Nicholas, a *Cornish* Man, Commander, bound for *Surat*.
We had a very prosperous Gale till we arrived at the *Cape* of
Good-hope, where we landed for fresh Water; but discovering
a Leak we unshipped our Goods, and wintered there; for the
Captain falling sick of an Ague, we could not leave the *Cape*
till the End of *March*. We then set sail, and had a good Voyage
till we passed the *Streights* of *Madagascar*; but having got
Northward of that Island, and to about five Degrees South
Latitude, the Winds, which in those Seas are observed to blow
a constant equal Gale between the North and West, from the
Beginning of *December* to the Beginning of *May*, on the 19th
of *April* began to blow with much greater Violence, and more
Westerly than usual; continuing so for twenty Days together,
during which time we were driven a little to the East of the
Molucca Islands, and about three Degrees Northward of the
Line, as our Captain found by an Observation he took the 2d
of *May*, at which time the Wind ceased, and it was a perfect
Calm, whereat I was not a little rejoyced. But he being a Man
well experienced in the Navigation of those Seas, bid us all

prepare against a Storm, which accordingly happened the Day following : For a Southern Wind, called the Southern *Monsoon*, began to set in.

Finding it was like to overblow, we took in our Spritsail, and stood by to hand the Fore-sail ; but making foul Weather, we looked the Guns were all fast, and handed the Missen. The Ship lay very broad off, so we thought it better spooning before the Sea, than trying or hulling. We reeft the Foresail and set him, we hawled aft the Foresheet ; the Helm was hard a Weather. The Ship wore bravely. We belay'd the Foredownhall ; but the Sail was split, and we hawl'd down the Yard, and got the Sail into the Ship, and unbound all the things clear of it. It was a very fierce Storm ; the Sea broke strange and dangerous. We hawl'd off upon the Lanniard of the Wipstaff, and helped the Man at Helm. We would not get down our Top-Mast, but let all stand, because she scudded before the Sea very well, and we knew that the Top-Mast being aloft, the Ship was the wholesomer, and made better way through the Sea, seeing we had Sea room. When the Storm was over, we set Fore-sail and Main-sail, and brought the Ship too. Then we set the Missen, Maintop-Sail and the Foretop-Sail. Our Course was East North-east, the Wind was at South-west. We got the Star-board Tack aboard, we cast off our Weatherbraces and Lifts ; we set in the Lee-braces, and hawl'd forward by the Weather-bowlings, and hawl'd them tight, and belayed them, and hawl'd over the Missen Tack to Windward, and kept her full and by as near as she would lye.

During this Storm, which was followed by a strong Wind West South-west, we were carried by my Computation about five hundred Leagues to the East, so that the oldest Sailor on Board could not tell in what part of the World we were. Our Provisions held out well, our Ship was staunch, and our Crew all in good Health ; but we lay in the utmost Distress for Water. We thought it best to hold on the same Course rather than turn more Northerly, which might have brought us to the North-west Parts of great *Tartary*, and into the frozen Sea.

On the 16*th* Day of *June* 1703, a Boy on the Top-mast discovered Land. On the 17*th* we came in full View of a great Island or Continent, (for we knew not whether) on the South-

side whereof was a small Neck of Land jutting out into the
Sea, and a Creek too shallow to hold a Ship of above one
hundred Tuns. We cast Anchor within a League of this
Creek, and our Captain sent a dozen of his Men well armed
in the Long Boat, with Vessels for Water if any could be
found. I desired his leave to go with them, that I might see
the Country, and make what Discoveries I could. When we
came to Land we saw no River or Spring, nor any Sign of
Inhabitants. Our Men therefore wandered on the Shore to
find out some fresh Water near the Sea, and I walked alone
about a Mile on the other Side, where I observed the Country
all barren and rocky. I now began to be weary, and seeing
nothing to entertain my Curiosity, I returned gently down
towards the Creek; and the Sea being full in my View, I saw
our Men already got into the Boat, and rowing for Life to
the Ship. I was going to hollow after them, although it had
been to little purpose, when I observed a huge Creature walking
after them in the Sea, as fast as he could : He walked not much
deeper than his Knees, and took prodigious strides : But our
Men had the start of him half a League, and the Sea thereabouts
being full of sharp pointed Rocks, the Monster was not able
to overtake the Boat. This I was afterwards told, for I durst
not stay to see the Issue of that Adventure ; but ran as fast as I
could the Way I first went ; and then climbed up a steep Hill,
which gave me some Prospect of the Country. I found it fully
cultivated ; but that which first surprized me was the Length
of the Grass, which in those Grounds that seemed to be kept
for Hay, was above twenty Foot high.

I fell into a high Road, for so I took it to be, although it
served to the Inhabitants only as a foot Path through a Field
of Barley. Here I walked on for some time, but could see little
on either Side, it being now near Harvest, and the Corn rising
at least Forty Foot. I was an Hour walking to the end of this
Field ; which was fenced in with a Hedge of at least one
hundred and twenty Foot high, and the Trees so lofty that I
could make no Computation of their Altitude. There was a
Stile to pass from this Field into the next : It had four Steps,
and a Stone to cross over when you came to the utmost. It was
impossible for me to climb this Stile, because every Step was

six Foot high, and the upper Stone above twenty. I was endeavouring to find some Gap in the Hedge; when I discovered one of the Inhabitants in the next Field advancing towards the Stile, of the same Size with him whom I saw in the Sea pursuing our Boat. He appeared as Tall as an ordinary Spire-steeple; and took about ten Yards at every Stride, as near as I could guess. I was struck with the utmost Fear and Astonishment, and ran to hide my self in the Corn, from whence I saw him at the Top of the Stile, looking back into the next Field on the right Hand; and heard him call in a Voice many Degrees louder than a speaking Trumpet; but the Noise was so High in the Air, that at first I certainly thought it was Thunder. Whereupon seven Monsters like himself came towards him with Reaping-Hooks in their Hands, each Hook about the largeness of six Scythes. These People were not so well clad as the first, whose Servants or Labourers they seemed to be. For, upon some Words he spoke, they went to reap the Corn in the Field where I lay. I kept from them at as great a Distance as I could, but was forced to move with extream Difficulty; for the Stalks of the Corn were sometimes not above a Foot distant, so that I could hardly squeeze my Body betwixt them. However, I made a shift to go forward till I came to a part of the Field where the Corn had been laid by the Rain and Wind: Here it was impossible for me to advance a step; for the Stalks were so interwoven that I could not creep through, and the Beards of the fallen Ears so strong and pointed, that they pierced through my Cloaths into my Flesh. At the same time I heard the Reapers not above an hundred Yards behind me. Being quite dispirited with Toil, and wholly overcome by Grief and Despair, I lay down between two Ridges, and heartily wished I might there end my Days. I bemoaned my desolate Widow, and Fatherless Children: I lamented my own Folly and Wilfulness in attempting a second Voyage against the Advice of all my Friends and Relations. In this terrible Agitation of Mind I could not forbear thinking of *Lilliput*, whose Inhabitants looked upon me as the greatest Prodigy that ever appeared in the World; where I was able to draw an Imperial Fleet in my Hand, and perform those other Actions which will be recorded for ever in the Chronicles of that Empire, while Posterity shall hardly believe them, although attested by Millions. I reflected what a Mortification it must prove to me to appear as inconsiderable in this Nation, as one single *Lilliputian* would be among us. But, this I conceived was to be the least of my Misfortunes : For, as human Creatures are observed to be more Savage and cruel in Proportion to their Bulk ; what could I expect but to, be a Morsel in the Mouth of the first among these enormous Barbarians who should happen to seize me ? Undoubtedly Philosophers are in the Right when they tell us, that nothing is great or little otherwise than by Comparison : It might have pleased Fortune to let the *Lilliputians* find some Nation, where the People were as diminutive with respect to them, as they were to me. And who knows but that even this prodigious Race of Mortals might be equally overmatched in some distant Part of the World, whereof we have yet no Discovery ?

Scared and confounded as I was, I could not forbear going on with these Reflections ; when one of the Reapers approaching within ten Yards of the Ridge where I lay, made me apprehend that with the next Step I should be squashed to Death under his Foot, or cut in two with his Reaping Hook. And therefore when he was again about to move, I screamed as loud as Fear could make me. Whereupon the huge Creature trod short, and looking round about under him for some time, at last espied me as I lay on the Ground. He considered a while with the Caution of one who endeavours to lay hold on a small dangerous Animal in such a Manner that it shall not be able either to scratch or to bite him ; as I my self have sometimes done with a *Weasel* in *England*. At length he ventured to take me up behind by the middle between his Fore-finger and Thumb, and brought me within three Yards of his Eyes, that he might behold my Shape more perfectly. I guessed his Meaning ; and my good Fortune gave me so much Presence of Mind, that I resolved not to struggle in the least as he held me in the Air above sixty Foot from the Ground ; although he grievously pinched my Sides, for fear I should slip through his Fingers. All I ventured was to raise my Eyes towards the Sun, and place my Hands together in a supplicating Posture, and to speak some Words in an humble melancholy Tone, suitable to the Condition I then was in. For, I apprehended every Moment that he would dash me against the Ground, as we usually do any little hateful Animal which we have a Mind to destroy. But my good Star would have it, that he appeared pleased with my Voice and Gestures, and began to look upon me as a Curiosity; much wondering to hear me pronounce articulate Words, although he could not understand them. In the mean time I was not able to forbear Groaning and shedding Tears, and turning my Head towards my Sides; letting him know, as well as I could, how cruelly I was hurt by the Pressure of his Thumb and Finger. He seemed to apprehend my Meaning; for, lifting up the Lappet of his Coat, he put me gently into it, and immediately ran along with me to his Master, who was a substantial Farmer, and the same Person I·had first seen in the Field.

The Farmer having (as I supposed by their Talk) received such an Account of me as his Servant could give him, took a piece of a small Straw, about the Size of a walking Staff, and therewith lifted up the Lappets of my Coat; which it seems he thought to be some kind of Covering that Nature had given me. He blew my Hairs aside to take a better View of my Face. He called his Hinds about him, and asked them (as I afterwards learned) whether they had ever seen in the Fields any little Creature that resembled me. He then placed me softly on the Ground upon all four; but I got immediately up, and walked slowly backwards and forwards, to let those People see I had no Intent to run away. They all sate down in a Circle about me, the better to observe my Motions. I pulled off my Hat, and made a low Bow towards the Farmer: I fell on my Knees, and lifted up my Hands and Eyes, and spoke several Words as loud as I could: I took a Purse of Gold out of my Pocket, and humbly presented it to him. He received it on the Palm of his Hand, then applied it close to his Eye, to see what it was, and afterwards turned it several times with the Point of a Pin, (which he took out of his Sleeve,) but could make nothing of it. Whereupon I made a Sign that he should place his Hand on the Ground: I then took the Purse, and opening it, poured all the Gold into his Palm. There were six *Spanish*-Pieces of four Pistoles each, besides twenty or thirty smaller

Coins. I saw him wet the Tip of his little Finger upon his Tongue, and take up one of my largest Pieces, and then another; but he seemed to be wholly ignorant what they were. He made me a Sign to put them again into my Purse, and the Purse again into my Pocket; which after offering to him several times, I thought it best to do.

The Farmer by this time was convinced I must be a rational Creature. He spoke often to me, but the Sound of his Voice pierced my Ears like that of a Water-Mill; yet his Words were articulate enough. I answered as loud as I could in several Languages; and he often laid his Ear within two Yards of me, but all in vain, for we were wholly unintelligible to each other. He then sent his Servants to their Work, and taking his Handkerchief out of his Pocket, he doubled and spread it on his Hand, which he placed flat on the Ground, with the Palm upwards, making me a Sign to step into it, as I could easily do, for it was not above a Foot in thickness. I thought it my part to obey; and for fear of falling, laid my self at full Length upon the Handkerchief, with the Remainder of which he lapped me up to the Head for further Security; and in this Manner carried me home to his House. There he called his Wife, and shewed me to her; but she screamed and ran back as Women in *England* do at the Sight of a Toad or a Spider. However, when she had a while seen my Behaviour, and how well I observed the Signs her Husband made, she was soon reconciled, and by Degrees grew extreamly tender of me.

It was about twelve at Noon, and a Servant brought in Dinner. It was only one substantial Dish of Meat (fit for the plain Condition of an Husband-Man) in a Dish of about four and twenty Foot Diameter. The Company were the Farmer and Wife, three Children, and an old Grandmother: When they were sat down, the Farmer placed me at some Distance from him on the Table, which was thirty Foot high from the Floor. I was in a terrible Fright, and kept as far as I could from the Edge, for fear of falling. The Wife minced a bit of Meat, then crumbled some Bread on a Trencher, and placed it before me. I made her a low Bow, took out my Knife and Fork, and fell to eat; which gave them exceeding Delight. The Mistress sent her Maid for a small Dram-cup, which held about two Gallons; and filled it with Drink: I took up the Vessel with much Difficulty in both Hands, and in a most respectful Manner drank to her Lady-ship's Health, expressing the Words as loud as I could in *English*; which made the Company laugh so heartily, that I was almost deafened with the Noise. This Liquour tasted like a small Cyder, and was not unpleasant. Then the Master made me a Sign to come to his Trencher side; but as I walked on the Table, being in great surprize all the time, as the indulgent Reader will easily conceive and excuse, I happened to stumble against a Crust, and fell flat on my Face, but received no hurt. I got up immediately, and observing the good People to be in much Concern, I took my Hat (which I held under my Arm out of good Manners) and waving it over my Head, made three Huzza's, to shew I had got no Mischief by the Fall. But advancing forwards towards my Master (as I shall henceforth call him) his youngest Son who sate next him, an arch Boy of about ten Years old, took me up by the Legs, and held me so high in the Air, that I trembled every Limb; but his Father snatched me from him; and at the same time gave him such a Box on the left Ear, as would have felled an *European* Troop of Horse to the Earth; ordering him to be taken from the Table. But, being afraid the Boy might owe me a Spight; and well remembering how mischievous all Children among us naturally are to Sparrows, Rabbits, young Kittens, and Puppy-Dogs; I fell on my Knees, and pointing to the Boy, made my Master understand, as well as I could, that I desired his Son might be pardoned. The Father complied, and the Lad took his Seat again; whereupon I went to him and kissed his Hand, which my Master took, and made him stroak me gently with it.

In the Midst of Dinner my Mistress's favourite Cat leapt into her Lap. I heard a Noise behind me like that of a Dozen Stocking-Weavers at work; and turning my Head, I found it proceeded from the Purring of this Animal, who seemed to be three Times larger than an Ox, as I computed by the View of her Head, and one of her Paws, while her Mistress was feeding and stroaking her. The Fierceness of this Creature's Countenance altogether discomposed me; although I stood at the further End of the Table, above fifty Foot off; and although my

Mistress held her fast for fear she might give a Spring, and seize me in her Talons. But it happened there was no Danger; for the Cat took not the least Notice of me when my Master placed me within three Yards of her. And as I have been always told, and found true by Experience in my Travels, that flying, or discovering Fear before a fierce Animal, is a certain Way to make it pursue or attack you; so I resolved in this dangerous Juncture to shew no Manner of Concern. I walked with Intrepidity five or six Times before the very Head of the Cat, and came within half a Yard of her; whereupon she drew her self back, as if she were more afraid of me: I had less Apprehension concerning the Dogs, whereof three or four came into the Room, as it is usual in Farmers Houses; one of which was a Mastiff equal in Bulk to four Elephants, and a Greyhound somewhat taller than the Mastiff, but not so large.

When Dinner was almost done, the Nurse came in with a Child of a Year old in her Arms; who immediately spyed me, and began a Squall that you might have heard from *London-Bridge* to *Chelsea*; after the usual Oratory of Infants, to get me for a Play-thing. The Mother out of pure Indulgence took me up, and put me towards the Child, who presently seized me by the Middle, and got my Head in his Mouth, where I roared so loud that the Urchin was frighted, and let me drop; and I should infallibly have broke my Neck, if the Mother had not held her Apron under me.

When the Dinner was done, my Master went out to his Labourers; and as I could discover by his Voice and Gesture, gave his Wife a strict Charge to take Care of me. I was very much tired and disposed to sleep, which my Mistress perceiving, she put me on her own Bed, and covered me with a clean white Handkerchief, but larger and coarser than the Main Sail of a Man of War.

I slept about two Hours, and dreamed I was at home with my Wife and Children, which aggravated my Sorrows when I awaked and found my self alone in a vast Room, between two and three Hundred Foot wide, and above two Hundred high; lying in a Bed twenty Yards wide. My Mistress was gone about her household Affairs, and had locked me in. The Bed was eight Yards from the Floor. I durst not presume to call, and if I had, it would have been in vain with such a Voice as mine at so great a Distance from the Room where I lay, to the Kitchen where the Family kept. While I was under these Circumstances, two Rats crept up the Curtains, and ran smelling backwards and forwards on the Bed : One of them came up almost to my Face ; whereupon I rose in a Fright, and drew out my Hanger to defend my self. These horrible Animals had the Boldness to attack me on both Sides, and one of them held his Fore-feet at my Collar ; but I had the good Fortune to rip up his Belly before he could do me any Mischief. He fell down at my Feet ; and the other seeing the Fate of his Comrade, made his Escape, but not without one good Wound on the Back, which I gave him as he fled, and made the Blood run trickling from him. After this Exploit I walked gently to and fro on the Bed, to recover my Breath and Loss of Spirits. These Creatures were of the Size of a large Mastiff, but infinitely more nimble and fierce ; so that if I had taken off my Belt before I went to sleep, I must have infallibly been torn to Pieces and devoured. I measured the Tail of the dead Rat, and found it to be two Yards long, wanting an Inch ; but it went against my Stomach to drag the Carcass off the Bed, where it lay still bleeding ; I observed it had yet some Life, but with a strong Slash cross the Neck, I thoroughly dispatched it.

Soon after, my Mistress came into the Room, who seeing me all bloody, ran and took me up in her Hand. I pointed to the dead *Rat*, smiling and making other Signs to shew I was not hurt ; whereat she was extremely rejoyced, calling the Maid to take up the dead *Rat* with a Pair of Tongs, and throw it out of the Window. Then she set me on a Table, where I shewed her my Hanger all bloody, and wiping it on the Lappet of my Coat, returned it to the Scabbard.

CHAPTER TWO

A DESCRIPTION OF THE FARMER'S DAUGHTER. THE AUTHOR CARRIED
TO A MARKET-TOWN, AND THEN TO THE METROPOLIS. THE
PARTICULARS OF HIS JOURNEY.

My Mistress had a Daughter of nine Years old, a Child of towardly Parts for her Age, very dextrous at her Needle, and skilful in dressing her Baby. Her Mother and she contrived to fit up the Baby's Cradle for me against Night : The Cradle was put into a small Drawer of a Cabinet, and the Drawer placed upon a hanging Shelf for fear of the *Rats*. This was my Bed all the Time I stayed with those People, although made more convenient by Degrees, as I began to learn their Language, and make my Wants known. This young Girl was so handy, that after I had once or twice pulled off my Cloaths before her, she was able to dress and undress me, although I never gave her that Trouble when she would let me do either my self. She made me seven Shirts, and some other Linnen of as fine Cloth as could be got, which indeed was coarser than Sackcloth ; and these she constantly washed for me with her own Hands. She was likewise my School-Mistress to teach me the Language : When I pointed to any thing, she told me the Name of it in her own Tongue, so that in a few Days I was able to call for whatever I had a mind to. She was very good natured, and not above forty Foot high, being little for her Age. She gave me the Name of *Grildrig*, which the Family took up, and afterwards the whole Kingdom. The Word imports what the *Latins* call *Nanunculus*, the *Italians Homunceletino*, and the *English Mannikin*. To her I chiefly owe my Preservation in that Country : We never parted while I was there ; I called her my *Glumdalclitch*, or little Nurse : And I should be guilty of great Ingratitude if I omitted this honourable Mention of her Care and Affection towards me, which I heartily wish it lay in my Power to requite as she deserves, instead of being the innocent but unhappy Instrument of her Disgrace, as I have too much Reason to fear.

It now began to be known and talked of in the Neighbourhood, that my Master had found a strange Animal in the Fields, about the Bigness of a *Splacknuck*, but exactly shaped in every Part like a human Creature; which it likewise imitated in all its Actions; seemed to speak in a little Language of its own, had already learned several Words of theirs, went erect upon two Legs, was tame and gentle, would come when it was called, do whatever it was bid, had the finest Limbs in the World, and a Complexion fairer than a Nobleman's Daughter of three Years old. Another Farmer who lived hard by, and was a particular Friend of my Master, came on a Visit on Purpose to enquire into the Truth of this Story. I was immediately produced, and placed upon a Table; where I walked as I was commanded, drew my Hanger, put it up again, made my Reverence to my Master's Guest, asked him in his own Language how he did, and told him he was welcome; just as my little Nurse had instructed me. This Man, who was old and dim-sighted, put on his Spectacles to behold me better, at which I could not forbear laughing very heartily; for his Eyes appeared like the Full-Moon shining into a Chamber at two Windows. Our People, who discovered the Cause of my Mirth, bore me Company in Laughing; at which the old Fellow was Fool enough to be angry and out of Countenance. He had the Character of a great Miser; and to my Misfortune he well deserved it by the cursed Advice he gave my Master, to shew me as a Sight upon a Market-Day in the next Town, which was half an Hour's Riding, about two and twenty Miles from our House. I guessed there was some Mischief contriving, when I observed my Master and his Friend whispering long together, sometimes pointing at me; and my Fears made me fancy that I overheard and undertood some of their Words. But, the next Morning *Glumdalclitch* my little Nurse told me the whole Matter, which she had cunningly picked out from her Mother. The poor Girl laid me on her Bosom, and fell a weeping with Shame and Grief. She apprehended some Mischief would happen to me from rude vulgar Folks, who might squeeze me to Death, or break one of my Limbs by taking me in their

Hands. She had also observed how modest I was in my Nature,
how nicely I regarded my Honour; and what an Indignity I
should conceive it to be exposed for Money as a publick
Spectacle to the meanest of the People. She said, her *Papa*
and *Mamma* had promised that *Grildrig* should be hers; but
now she found they meant to serve her as they did last Year,
when they pretended to give her a Lamb; and yet, as soon as
it was fat, sold it to a Butcher. For my own Part, I may truly
affirm that I was less concerned than my Nurse. I had a strong
Hope which never left me, that I should one Day recover my
Liberty.

My Master, pursuant of the Advice of his Friend, carried me
in a Box the next Market-Day to the neighbouring Town; and
took along with him his little Daughter my Nurse upon a
Pillion behind me. The Box was close on every Side, with a
little Door for me to go in and out, and a few Gimlet-holes to
let in Air. The Girl had been so careful to put the Quilt of her
Baby's Bed into it, for me to lye down on. However, I was
terribly shaken and discomposed in this Journey, although it
were but of half an Hour. For the Horse went about forty
Foot at every Step; and trotted so high, that the Agitation was
equal to the rising and falling of a Ship in a great Storm, but
much more frequent: Our Journey was somewhat further than
from *London* to St. *Albans*. My Master alighted at an Inn
which he used to frequent; and after consulting a while with
the Inn-keeper, and making some necessary Preparations, he
hired the *Grultrud*, or Cryer, to give Notice through the Town,
of a strange Creature to be seen at the Sign of the Green *Eagle*,
not so big as a *Splacknuck*, (an Animal in that Country very
finely shaped, about six Foot long) and in every Part of the
Body resembling an human Creature; could speak several
Words, and perform an Hundred diverting Tricks.

I was placed upon a Table in the largest Room of the Inn,
which might be near three Hundred Foot square. My little
Nurse stood on a low Stool close to the Table, to take care of
me, and direct what I should do. My Master, to avoid a Croud,
would suffer only Thirty People at a Time to see me. I walked
about on the Table as the Girl commanded; she asked me
Questions as far as she knew my Understanding of the Language

reached, and I answered them as loud as I could. I turned
about several Times to the Company, paid my humble Respects,
said they were welcome; and used some other Speeches I had
been taught. I took up a Thimble filled with Liquor, which
Glumdalclitch had given me for a Cup, and drank their Health.
I drew out my Hanger, and flourished with it after the Manner
of Fencers in *England*. My Nurse gave me Part of a Straw,
which I exercised as a Pike, having learned the Art in my
Youth. I was that Day shewn to twelve Sets of Company; and
as often forced to go over again with the same Fopperies, till
I was half dead with Weariness and Vexation. For, those who
had seen me, made such wonderful Reports, that the People
were ready to break down the Doors to come in. My Master
for his own Interest would not suffer any one to touch me,
except my Nurse; and, to prevent Danger, Benches were set
round the Table at such a Distance, as put me out of every
Body's Reach. However, an unlucky School-Boy aimed a
Hazel-Nut directly at my Head, which very narrowly missed
me; otherwise, it came with so much Violence, that it would
have infallibly knocked out my Brains; for it was almost as
large as a small Pumpion: But I had the Satisfaction to see the
young Rogue well beaten, and turned out of the Room.

My Master gave publick Notice, that he would shew me
again the next Market-Day: And in the mean time, he prepared a more convenient Vehicle for me, which he had Reason
enough to do; for I was so tired with my first Journey, and
with entertaining Company eight Hours together, that I could
hardly stand upon my Legs, or speak a Word. It was at least
three Days before I recovered my Strength; and that I might
have no rest at home, all the neighbouring Gentlemen from an
Hundred Miles round, hearing of my Fame, came to see me at
my Master's own House. There could not be fewer than thirty
Persons with their Wives and Children; (for the Country is
very populous;) and my Master demanded the Rate of a
full Room whenever he shewed me at Home, although it were
only to a single Family. So that for some time I had but little
Ease every Day of the Week, (except *Wednesday*, which is
their Sabbath) although I were not carried to the Town.

My Master finding how profitable I was like to be, resolved

to carry me to the most considerable Cities of the Kingdom. Having therefore provided himself with all things necessary for a long Journey, and settled his Affairs at Home; he took Leave of his Wife; and upon the 17th of *August* 1703, about two Months after my Arrival, we set out for the Metropolis, situated near the Middle of that Empire, and about three Thousand Miles distance from our House: My Master made his Daughter *Glumdalclitch* ride behind him. She carried me on her Lap in a Box tied about her Waist. The Girl had lined it on all Sides with the softest Cloth she could get, well quilted underneath; furnished it with her Baby's Bed, provided me with Linnen and other Necessaries; and made every thing as convenient as she could. We had no other Company but a Boy of the House, who rode after us with the Luggage.

My Master's Design was to shew me in all the Towns by the Way, and to step out of the Road for Fifty or an Hundred Miles, to any Village or Person of Quality's House where he might expect Custom. We made easy Journies of not above seven or eight Score Miles a Day: For *Glumdalclitch*, on Purpose to spare me, complained she was tired with the trotting of the Horse. She often took me out of my Box at my own Desire, to give me Air, and shew me the Country; but always held me fast by Leading-strings. We passed over five or six Rivers many Degrees broader and deeper than the *Nile* or the *Ganges*; and there was hardly a Rivulet so small as the *Thames* at *London-Bridge*. We were ten Weeks in our Journey; and I was shewn in Eighteen large Towns, besides many Villages and private Families.

On the 26th Day of *October*, we arrived at the Metropolis, called in their Language *Lorbrulgrud*, or *Pride of the Universe*. My Master took a Lodging in the principal Street of the City, not far from the Royal Palace; and put out Bills in the usual Form, containing an exact Description of my Person and Parts. I was shewn ten Times a Day to the Wonder and Satisfaction of all People. I could now speak the Language tolerably well; and perfectly understood every Word that was spoken to me. Besides, I had learned their Alphabet, and could make a shift to explain a Sentence here and there; for *Glumdalclitch* had been my Instructer while we were at home, and at leisure

Hours during our Journey. She carried a little Book in her Pocket, not much larger than a *Sanson's Atlas*; it was a common Treatise for the use of young Girls, giving a short Account of their Religion; out of this she taught me my Letters, and interpreted the Words.

CHAPTER THREE

THE AUTHOR SENT FOR TO COURT. THE QUEEN BUYS HIM OF HIS MASTER THE FARMER, AND PRESENTS HIM TO THE KING. HE DISPUTES WITH HIS MAJESTY'S GREAT SCHOLARS. AN APARTMENT AT COURT PROVIDED FOR THE AUTHOR. HE IS IN HIGH FAVOUR WITH THE QUEEN. HIS QUARRELS WITH THE QUEEN'S DWARF.

THE frequent Labours I underwent every Day, made in a few Weeks a very considerable Change in my Health: The more my Master got by me, the more unsatiable he grew. I had quite lost my Stomach, and was almost reduced to a Skeleton. The Farmer observed it; and concluding I soon must die, resolved to make as good a Hand of me as he could. While he was thus reasoning and resolving with himself; a *Slardral*, or Gentleman Usher, came from Court, commanding my Master to bring me immediately thither for the Diversion of the Queen and her Ladies. Some of the latter had already been to see me; and reported strange Things of my Beauty, Behaviour, and good Sense. Her Majesty and those who attended her, were beyond Measure delighted with my Demeanor. I fell on my Knees, and begged the Honour of kissing her Imperial Foot; but this Gracious Princess held out her little Finger towards me (after I was set on a Table) which I embraced in both my Arms, and put the Tip of it, with the utmost Respect, to my Lip. She made me some general Questions about my Country and my Travels, which I answered as distinctly and in as few Words as I could. She asked, whether I would be content to live at Court. I bowed down to the Board of the Table, and humbly answered, that I was my

Master's Slave; but if I were at my own Disposal, I should be proud to devote my Life to her Majesty's Service. She then asked my Master whether he were willing to sell me at a good Price. He, who apprehended I could not live a Month, was ready enough to part with me; and demanded a Thousand Pieces of Gold; which were ordered him on the Spot, each Piece being about the Bigness of eight Hundred Moydores: But, allowing for the Proportion of all Things between that Country and *Europe*, and the high Price of Gold among them; was hardly so great a Sum as a Thousand Guineas would be in *England*. I then said to the Queen; since I was now her Majesty's most humble Creature and Vassal, I must beg the Favour, that *Glumdalclitch*, who had always tended me with so much Care and Kindness, and understood to do it so well, might be admitted into her Service, and continue to be my Nurse and Instructor. Her Majesty agreed to my Petition; and easily got the Farmer's Consent, who was glad enough to have his Daughter preferred at Court: And the poor Girl herself was not able to hide her Joy. My late Master withdrew, bidding me farewell, and saying he had left me in a good Service; to which I replyed not a Word, only making him a slight Bow.

The Queen observed my Coldness; and when the Farmer was gone out of the Apartment, asked me the Reason. I made bold to tell her Majesty, that I owed no other Obligation to my late Master, than his not dashing out the Brains of a poor harmless Creature found by Chance in his Field; which Obligation was amply recompenced by the Gain he had made in shewing me through half the Kingdom, and the Price he had now sold me for. That the Life I had since led, was laborious enough to kill an Animal of ten Times my Strength. That my Health was much impaired by the continual Drudgery of entertaining the Rabble every Hour of the Day; and that if my Master had not thought my Life in Danger, her Majesty perhaps would not have got so cheap a Bargain. But as I was out of all fear of being ill treated under the Protection of so great and good an Empress, the Ornament of Nature, the Darling of the World, the Delight of her Subjects, the Phoenix of the Creation; so, I hoped my late Master's Apprehensions would appear to be groundless; for I already found my Spirits to revive by the Influence of her most August Presence.

The Queen giving great Allowance for my Defectiveness in speaking, was however surprised at so much Wit and good Sense in so diminutive an Animal. She took me in her own Hand, and carried me to the King, who was then retired to his Cabinet. His Majesty, a Prince of much Gravity, and austere Countenance, not well observing my Shape at first View, asked the Queen after a cold Manner, how long it was since she grew fond of a *Splacknuck*; for such it seems he took me to be, as I lay upon my Breast in her Majesty's right Hand. But this Princess, who hath an infinite deal of Wit and Humour, set me gently on my Feet upon the Scrutore; and commanded me to give His Majesty an Account of my self, which I did in a very few Words; and *Glumdalclitch*, who attended at the Cabinet Door, and could not endure I should be out of her Sight, being admitted; confirmed all that had passed from my Arrival at her Father's House.

The King, although he be as learned a Person as any in his Dominions; and had been educated in the Study of Philosophy, and particularly Mathematicks; yet when he observed my Shape exactly, and saw me walk erect, before I began to speak, conceived I might be a piece of Clockwork, (which is in that Country arrived to a very great Perfection) contrived by some ingenious Artist. But, when he heard my Voice, and found what I delivered to be regular and rational, he could not conceal his Astonishment. He was by no means satisfied with the Relation I gave him of the Manner I came into his Kingdom; but thought it a Story concerted between *Glumdalclitch* and her Father, who had taught me a Sett of Words to make me sell at a higher Price. Upon this Imagination he put several other Questions to me, and still received rational Answers, no otherwise defective than by a Foreign Accent, and an imperfect Knowledge in the Language; with some rustick Phrases which I had learned at the Farmer's House, and did not suit the polite Style of a Court.

I applied my self to the King, and assured His Majesty, that I came from a Country which abounded with several Millions of both Sexes, and of my own Stature; where the Animals,

Trees, and Houses were all in Proportion; and where by
Consequence I might be as able to defend my self, and to find
Sustenance, as any of his Majesty's Subjects could do here.
To this they only replied with a Smile of Contempt; saying,
that the Farmer had instructed me very well in my Lesson. The
King, who had a much better Understanding, dismissing his
learned Men, sent for the Farmer, who by good Fortune was
not yet gone out of Town: Having therefore first examined
him privately, and then confronted him with me and the
young Girl; his Majesty began to think that what we told him
might possibly be true. He desired the Queen to order, that
a particular Care should be taken of me; and was of Opinion,
that *Glumdalclitch* should still continue in her Office of tending
me, because he observed we had a great Affection for each
other. A convenient Apartment was provided for her at Court;
she had a sort of Governess appointed to take care of her
Education, a Maid to dress her, and two other Servants for
menial Offices; but, the Care of me was wholly appropriated
to her self. The Queen commanded her own Cabinet-maker
to contrive a Box that might serve me for a Bed-chamber, after
the Model that *Glumdalclitch* and I should agree upon. This
Man was a most ingenious Artist; and according to my
Directions, in three Weeks finished for me a wooden Chamber
of sixteen Foot square, and twelve High; with Sash Windows,
a Door, and two Closets, like a *London* Bed-chamber. The
Board that made the Cieling was to be lifted up and down by
two Hinges, to put in a Bed ready furnished by her Majesty's
Upholsterer; which *Glumdalclitch* took out every Day to air,
made it with her own Hands, and letting it down at Night,
locked up the Roof over me. A Nice Workman, who was
famous for little Curiosities, undertook to make me two Chairs,
with Backs and Frames, of a Substance not unlike Ivory; and
two Tables, with a Cabinet to put my Things in. The Room
was quilted on all Sides, as well as the Floor and the Cieling,
to prevent any Accident from the Carelessness of those who
carried me; and to break the Force of a Jolt when I went
in a Coach. I desired a Lock for my Door to prevent Rats and
Mice from coming in: The Smith after several Attempts made
the smallest that ever was seen among them; for I have known

a larger at the Gate of a Gentleman's House in *England*. I made a shift to keep the Key in a Pocket of my own, fearing *Glumdalclitch* might lose it. The Queen likewise ordered the thinnest Silks that could be gotten, to make me Cloaths ; not much thicker than an *English* Blanket, very cumbersome till I was accustomed to them. They were after the Fashion of the Kingdom, partly resembling the *Persian*, and partly the *Chinese* ; and are a very grave decent Habit.

The Queen became so fond of my Company, that she could not dine without me. I had a Table placed upon the same at which her Majesty eat, just at her left Elbow ; and a Chair to sit on. *Glumdalclitch* stood upon a Stool on the Floor, near my Table, to assist and take Care of me. I had an entire set of Silver Dishes and Plates, and other Necessaries, which in Proportion to those of the Queen, were not much bigger than what I have seen in a *London* Toy-shop, for the Furniture of a Baby-house : These my little Nurse kept in her Pocket, in a Silver Box, and gave me at Meals as I wanted them ; always cleaning them her self. No Person dined with the Queen but the two Princesses Royal ; the elder sixteen Years old, and the younger at that time thirteen and a Month. Her Majesty used to put a Bit of Meat upon one of my Dishes, out of which I carved for my self ; and her Diversion was to see me eat in Miniature. For the Queen (who had indeed but a weak Stomach) took up at one Mouthful, as much as a dozen *English* Farmers could eat at a Meal, which to me was for some time a very nauseous Sight. She would craunch the Wing of a Lark, Bones and all, between her Teeth, although it were nine Times as large as that of a full grown Turkey ; and put a Bit of Bread in her Mouth, as big as two twelve-penny Loaves. She drank out of a Golden Cup, above a Hogshead at a Draught. Her Knives were twice as long as a Scythe set strait upon the Handle. The Spoons, Forks, and other Instruments were all in the same Proportion. I remember when *Glumdalclitch* carried me out of Curiosity to see some of the Tables at Court, where ten or a dozen of these enormous Knives and Forks were lifted up together ; I thought I had never till then beheld so terrible a Sight.

Nothing angered and mortified me so much as the Queen's

Dwarf, who being of the lowest Stature that was ever in that Country, (for I verily think he was not full Thirty Foot high) became so insolent at seeing a Creature so much beneath him, that he would always affect to swagger and look big as he passed by me in the Queen's Antichamber, while I was standing on some Table talking with the Lords or Ladies of the Court; and he seldom failed of a smart Word or two upon my Littleness; against which I could only revenge my self by calling him *Brother*, challenging him to wrestle; and such Repartees as are usual in the Mouths of *Court Pages*. One Day at Dinner, this malicious little Cubb was so nettled with something I had said to him, that raising himself upon the Frame of her Majesty's Chair, he took me up by the Middle, as I was sitting down, not thinking any Harm, and let me drop into a large Silver Bowl of Cream; and then ran away as fast as he could. I fell over Head and Ears, and if I had not been a good Swimmer, it might have gone very hard with me; for *Glumdalclitch* in that Instant happened to be at the other End of the Room; and the Queen was in such a Fright, that she wanted Presence of Mind to assist me. But my little Nurse ran to my Relief; and took me out, after I had swallowed above a Quart of Cream. I was put to Bed; however I received no other Damage than the Loss of a Suit of Cloaths, which was utterly spoiled. The Dwarf was soundly whipped, and as a further Punishment, forced to drink up the Bowl of Cream, into which he had thrown me; neither was he ever restored to Favour: For, soon after the Queen bestowed him to a Lady of high Quality; so that I saw him no more, to my very great Satisfaction; for I could not tell to what Extremitys such a malicious Urchin might have carried his Resentment.

He had before served me a scurvy Trick, which set the Queen a laughing, although at the same time she were heartily vexed, and would have immediately cashiered him, if I had not been so generous as to intercede. Her Majesty had taken a Marrow-bone upon her Plate; and after knocking out the Marrow, placed the Bone again in the Dish erect as it stood before; the Dwarf watching his Opportunity, while *Glumdalclitch* was gone to the Side-board, mounted the Stool that she stood on to take care of me at Meals; took me up in both

Hands, and squeezing my Legs together, wedged them into the Marrow-bone above my Waist; where I stuck for some time, and made a very ridiculous Figure. I believe it was near a Minute before any one knew what was become of me; for I thought it below me to cry out. But, as Princes seldom get their Meat hot, my Legs were not scalded, only my Stockings and Breeches in a sad Condition. The Dwarf at my Entreaty had no other Punishment than a sound whipping.

I was frequently raillied by the Queen upon Account of my Fearfulness; and she used to ask me whether the People of my Country were as great Cowards as my self. The Occasion was this. The Kingdom is much pestered with Flies in Summer; and these odious Insects, each of them as big as a *Dunstable* Lark, hardly gave me any Rest while I sat at Dinner, with their continual Humming and Buzzing about my Ears. I had much ado to defend my self against these detestable Animals, and could not forbear starting when they came on my Face. It was the common Practice of the Dwarf to catch a Number of these Insects in his Hand, as School-boys do among us, and let them out suddenly under my Nose, on Purpose to frighten me, and divert the Queen. My Remedy was to cut them in Pieces with my Knife as they flew in the Air; wherein my Dexterity was much admired.

I remember one Morning when *Glumdalclitch* had set me in my Box upon a Window, as she usually did in fair Days to give me Air, (for I durst not venture to let the Box be hung on a Nail out of the Window, as we do with Cages in *England*) after I had lifted up one of my Sashes, and sat down at my Table to eat a Piece of Sweet-Cake for my Breakfast; above twenty Wasps, allured by the Smell, came flying into the Room, humming louder than the Drones of as many Bagpipes. Some of them seized my Cake, and carried it piecemeal away; others flew about my Head and Face, confounding me with the Noise, and putting me in the utmost Terror of their Stings. However I had the Courage to rise and draw my Hanger, and attack them in the Air. I dispatched four of them, but the rest got away; and I presently shut my Window. These Insects were as large as Partridges; I took out their Stings, found them an Inch and a half long, and as sharp as Needles. I carefully preserved them all, and having since shewn them with some other Curiosities in several Parts of *Europe*; upon my Return to *England* I gave three of them to *Gresham College*, and kept the fourth for my self.

CHAPTER FOUR

THE COUNTRY DESCRIBED. THE KING'S PALACE, AND SOME ACCOUNT OF THE METROPOLIS. THE AUTHOR'S WAY OF TRAVELLING. THE CHIEF TEMPLE DESCRIBED.

I NOW intend to give the Reader a short Description of this Country, as far as I travelled in it, which was not above two thousand Miles round *Lorbrulgrud* the Metropolis. For, the Queen, whom I always attended, never went further when she accompanied the King in his Progresses; and there staid till his Majesty returned from viewing his Frontiers. The whole Extent of this Prince's Dominions reacheth about six thousand Miles in Length, and from three to five in Breadth. From whence I cannot but conclude, that our Geographers of *Europe* are in a great Error, by supposing nothing but Sea between *Japan* and *California*: For it was ever my Opinion, that there must be a Balance of Earth to counterpoise the great Continent of *Tartary*; and therefore they ought to correct their Maps and Charts, by joining this vast Tract of Land to the North-west Parts of *America*; wherein I shall be ready to lend them my Assistance.

The Kingdom is a Peninsula, terminated to the North-east by a Ridge of Mountains thirty Miles high which are altogether impassable by Reason of the Volcanoes upon the Tops. Neither do the most Learned know what sort of Mortals inhabit beyond those Mountains, or whether they be inhabited at all. On the three other Sides it is bounded by the Ocean. There is not one Sea-port in the whole Kingdom; and those Parts of the Coasts into which the Rivers issue, are so full of pointed Rocks, and the Sea generally so rough, that there is no venturing with the smallest of their Boats; so that these People are wholly excluded from any Commerce with the rest of the World. But the large Rivers are full of Vessels, and abound with excellent Fish; for they seldom get any from the Sea, because the Sea-fish are of the same Size with those in *Europe*, and consequently not worth catching; whereby it is manifest, that Nature in the Production of Plants and Animals of so extraordinary a Bulk, is wholly confined to this Continent; of which I leave the Reasons to be determined by Philosophers. However, now and then they take a Whale that happens to be dashed against the Rocks, which the common People feed on heartily. These Whales I have known so large that a Man could hardly carry one upon his Shoulders; and sometimes for Curiosity they are brought in Hampers to *Lorbrulgrud*: I saw one of them in a Dish at the King's Table, which passed for a Rarity; but I did not observe he was fond of it; for I think indeed the Bigness disgusted him, although I have seen one somewhat larger in *Greenland*.

The Country is well inhabited, for it contains fifty one Cities, near an hundred walled Towns, and a great Number of Villages. To satisfy my curious Reader, it may be sufficient to describe *Lorbrulgrud*. This City stands upon almost two equal Parts on each Side the River that passes through. It contains above eighty thousand Houses. It is in Length three *Glonglungs* (which make about fifty four English Miles) and two and a half in Breadth, as I measured it myself in the Royal Map made by the King's Order, which was laid on the Ground on purpose for me, and extended an hundred Feet; I paced the Diameter and Circumference several times Barefoot, and computing by the Scale, measured it pretty exactly.

The King's Palace is no regular Edifice, but an Heap of Buildings about seven Miles round: The chief Rooms are generally two hundred and forty Foot high, and broad and long in Proportion. A Coach was allowed to *Glumdalclitch* and me, wherein her Governess frequently took her out to see the Town, or go among the Shops; and I was always of the Party, carried in my Box; although the Girl at my own Desire would often take me out, and hold me in her Hand, that I might more conveniently view the Houses and the People as we passed

along the Streets. I reckoned our Coach to be about a Square
of *Westminster-Hall*, but not altogether so high; however, I
cannot be very exact.

Beside the large Box in which I was usually carried, the
Queen ordered a smaller one to be made for me, of about
twelve Foot Square, and ten high, for the Convenience of
Travelling; because the other was somewhat too large for
Glumdalclitch's Lap, and cumbersom in the Coach; it was
made by the same Artist, whom I directed in the whole Contrivance. This travelling Closet was an exact Square with a
Window in the Middle of three of the Squares, and each
Window was latticed with Iron Wire on the outside, to prevent
Accidents in long Journeys. On the fourth Side, which had
no Window, two strong Staples were fixed, through which the
Person that carried me, when I had a Mind to be on Horseback,
put in a Leathern Belt, and buckled it about his Waist. This
was always the Office of some grave trusty Servant in whom I
could confide, whether I attended the King and Queen in their
Progresses, or were disposed to see the Gardens, or pay a Visit
to some great Lady or Minister of State in the Court, when
Glumdalclitch happened to be out of Order: For I soon began
to be known and esteemed among the greatest Officers, I
suppose more upon Account of their Majesty's Favour, than
any Merit of my own. In Journeys, when I was weary of the
Coach, a Servant on Horseback would buckle my Box, and
place it on a Cushion before him; and there I had a full
Prospect of the Country on three Sides from my three Windows. I had in this Closet a Field-Bed and a Hammock hung
from the Ceiling, two Chairs and a Table, neatly screwed to
the Floor, to prevent being tossed about by the Agitation of
the Horse or the Coach. And having been long used to Sea-
Voyages, those Motions, although sometimes very violent, did
not much discompose me.

Whenever I had a Mind to see the Town, it was always in
my Travelling-Closet; which *Glumdalclitch* held in her Lap in
a kind of open Sedan, after the Fashion of the Country, born
by four Men, and attended by two others in the Queen's
Livery. The People who had often heard of me, were very
curious to croud about the Sedan; and the Girl was complaisant

enough to make the Bearers stop, and to take me in her Hand
that I might be more conveniently seen.

I was very desirous to see the chief Temple, and particularly
the Tower belonging to it, which is reckoned the highest in
in the Kingdom. Accordingly one Day my Nurse carried me
thither, but I may truly say I came back disappointed; for,
the Height is not above three thousand Foot, reckoning from
the Ground to the highest Pinnacle top; which allowing for
the Difference between the Size of those People, and us in
Europe, is no great matter for Admiration, nor at all equal in
Proportion, (if I rightly remember) to *Salisbury* Steeple. But,
not to detract from a Nation to which during my Life I shall
acknowledge myself extremely obliged; it must be allowed,
that whatever this famous Tower wants in Height, is amply
made up in Beauty and Strength. For the Walls are near an
hundred Foot thick, built of hewn Stone, whereof each is
about forty Foot square, and adorned on all Sides with Statues
of Gods and Emperors cut in Marble larger than the Life,
placed in their several Niches. I measured a little Finger which
had fallen down from one of these Statues, and lay unperceived
among some Rubbish; and found it exactly four Foot and an
Inch in Length. *Glumdalclitch* wrapped it up in a Handkerchief,
and carried it home in her Pocket to keep among other Trinkets,
of which the Girl was very fond, as Children at her Age usually
are.

The King's Kitchen is indeed a noble Building, vaulted at
Top, and about six hundred Foot high. The great Oven is not
so wide by ten Paces as the Cupola at St. *Paul's*: For I measured
the latter on purpose after my Return. But if I should describe
the Kitchen-grate, the prodigious Pots and Kettles, the Joints of
Meat turning on the Spits, with many other Particulars;
perhaps I should be hardly believed; at least a severe Critick
would be apt to think I enlarged a little, as Travellers are often
suspected to do.

His Majesty seldom keeps above six hundred Horses in his
Stables: They are generally from fifty four to sixty Foot high.
But, when he goes abroad on solemn Days, he is attended for
State by a Militia Guard of five hundred Horse, which indeed
I thought was the most splendid Sight that could be ever beheld.

CHAPTER FIVE

SEVERAL ADVENTURES THAT HAPPENED TO THE AUTHOR. THE
AUTHOR SHEWS HIS SKILL IN NAVIGATION.

I SHOULD have lived happy enough in that Country, if my
Littleness had not exposed me to several ridiculous and
troublesome Accidents ; some of which I shall venture to relate.
Glumdalclitch often carried me into the Gardens of the Court
in my smaller Box, and would sometimes take me out of it and
hold me in her Hand, or set me down to walk. I remember,
before the Dwarf left the Queen, he followed us one Day into
those Gardens ; and my Nurse having set me down, he and I
being close together, near some Dwarf Apple-trees, I must
need shew my Wit by a silly Allusion between him and the
Trees, which happens to hold in their Language as it doth in
ours. Whereupon, the malicious Rogue watching his Opportunity, when I was walking under one of them, shook it directly
over my Head, by which a dozen Apples, each of them near as
large as a *Bristol* Barrel, came tumbling about my Ears ; one
of them hit me on the Back as I chanced to stoop, and knocked
me down flat on my Face, but I received no other Hurt ; and
the Dwarf was pardoned at my Desire, because I had given the
Provocation.

Another Day, *Glumdalclitch* left me on a smooth Grass-plot
to divert my self while she walked at some Distance with her
Governess. In the mean time, there suddenly fell such a
violent Shower of Hail, that I was immediately by the Force
of it struck to the Ground : And when I was down, the Hail-
stones gave me such cruel Bangs all over the Body, as if I had
been pelted with Tennis-Balls ; however I made a Shift to
creep on all four, and shelter my self by lying flat on my Face
on the Lee-side of a Border of Lemmon Thyme ; but so
bruised from Head to Foot, that I could not go abroad in ten
Days. Neither is this at all to be wondered at ; because Nature
in that Country observing the same Proportion through all her

Operations, a Hail-stone is near Eighteen Hundred Times as large as one in *Europe*.

But, a more dangerous Accident happened to me in the same Garden, when my little Nurse, believing she had put me in a secure Place, which I often entreated her to do, that I might enjoy my own thoughts; and having left my Box at home to avoid the Trouble of carrying it, went to another Part of the Gardens with her Governess and some Ladies of her Acquaintance. While she was absent and out of hearing, a small white Spaniel belonging to one of the chief Gardiners, having got by Accident into the Garden, happened to range near the Place where I lay. The Dog following the Scent, came directly up, and taking me in his Mouth, ran strait to his Master, wagging his Tail, and set me gently on the Ground. By good Fortune he had been so well taught, that I was carried between his Teeth without the least Hurt, or even tearing my Cloaths. But, the poor Gardiner, who knew me well, and had a great Kindness for me, was in a terrible Fright. He gently took me up in both his Hands, and asked me how I did ; but I was so amazed and out of Breath, that I could not speak a Word. In a few Minutes I came to my self, and he carried me safe to my little Nurse, who by this time had returned to the Place where she had left me, and was in cruel Agonies when I did not appear, nor answer when she called ; she severely reprimanded the Gardiner on Account of his Dog. But, the Thing was hushed up, and never known at Court ; for the Girl was afraid of the Queen's Anger ; and truly as to my self, I thought it would not be for my Reputation that such a Story should go about.

This Accident absolutely determined *Glumdalclitch* never to trust me abroad for the future out of her Sight. I had been long afraid of this Resolution ; and therefore concealed from her some little unlucky Adventures that happened in those Times when I was left by my self. Once a Kite hovering over the Garden, made a Stoop at me, and if I had not resolutely drawn my Hanger, and run under a thick Espalier, he would have certainly carried me away in his Talons. Another time, walking to the Top of a fresh Mole-hill, I fell to my Neck, in the Hole through which that Animal had cast up the Earth; and coined some Lye not worth remembering, to excuse my self for spoiling my Cloaths. I likewise broke my right Shin against the Shell of a Snail, which I happened to stumble over, as I was walking alone, and thinking on poor *England*.

I cannot tell whether I were more pleased or mortified to observe in those solitary Walks, that the smaller Birds did not appear to be at all afraid of me; but would hop about within a Yard Distance, looking for Worms, and other Food, with as much Indifference and Security as if no Creature at all were near them. I remember, a Thrush had the Confidence to snatch out of my Hand with his Bill, a Piece of Cake that *Glumdalclitch* had just given me for my Breakfast. When I attempted to catch any of these Birds, they would boldly turn against me, endeavouring to pick my Fingers, which I durst not venture within their Reach; and then they would hop back unconcerned to hunt for Worms or Snails, as they did before. But, one Day I took a thick Cudgel, and threw it with all my Strength so luckily at a Linnet, that I knocked him down, and seizing him by the Neck with both my Hands, ran with him in Triumph to my Nurse. However, the Bird who had only been stunned, recovering himself, gave me so many Boxes with his Wings on both Sides of my Head and Body, although I held him at Arms Length, and was out of the Reach of his Claws, that I was twenty Times thinking to let him go. But I was soon relieved by one of our Servants, who wrung off the Bird's Neck; and I had him next Day for Dinner by the Queen's Command. This Linnet, as near as I can remember, seemed to be somewhat larger than an *English* Swan.

The Queen, who often used to hear me talk of my Sea-Voyages, and took all Occasions to divert me when I was melancholy, asked me whether I understood how to handle a Sail or an Oar; and whether a little Exercise of Rowing might not be convenient for my Health. I answered, that I understood both very well. For although my proper Employment had been to be a Surgeon or Doctor to the Ship; yet often upon a Pinch, I was forced to work like a common Mariner. But, I could not see how this could be done in their Country, where the smallest Wherry was equal to a first Rate Man of War among us; and such a Boat as I could manage would never live in any of the Rivers: Her Majesty said, if I would contrive

a Boat, her own Joyner should make it, and she would provide
a Place for me to sail in. The Fellow was an ingenious Workman, and by my Instructions in ten Days finished a Pleasure-
Boat with all its Tackling, able conveniently to hold eight
Europeans. When it was finished, the Queen was so delighted,
that she ran with it in her Lap to the King, who ordered it to
be put in a Cistern full of Water, with me in it, by way of
Tryal; where I could not manage my two Sculls or little
Oars for want of Room. But, the Queen had before contrived
another Project. She ordered the Joyner to make a wooden
Trough of three Hundred Foot long, fifty broad, and eight
deep; which being well pitched to prevent leaking, was placed
on the Floor along the Wall, in an outer Room of the Palace.
It had a Cock near the Bottom, to let out the Water when it
began to grow stale; and two Servants could easily fill it in
half an Hour. Here I often used to row for my Diversion, as
well as that of the Queen and her Ladies, who thought themselves agreeably entertained with my Skill and Agility. Sometimes I would put up my Sail, and then my Business was only
to steer, while the Ladies gave me a Gale with their Fans; and
when they were weary, some of the Pages would blow my Sail
forward with their Breath, while I shewed my Art by steering
Starboard or Larboard as I pleased. When I had done, *Glumdalclitch* always carried back my Boat into her Closet, and hung
it on a Nail to dry.

In this Exercise I once met an Accident which had like to
have cost me my Life. For, one of the Pages having put my
Boat into the Trough; the Governess who attended *Glumdalclitch*, very officiously lifted me up to place me in the Boat;
but I happened to slip through her Fingers, and should have
infallibly fallen down forty Foot upon the Floor, if by the
luckiest Chance in the World, I had not been stop'd by a
Corking-pin that stuck in the good Gentlewoman's Stomacher;
the Head of the Pin passed between my Shirt and the Waist-
band of my Breeches; and thus I was held by the Middle in
the Air, till *Glumdalclitch* ran to my Relief.

Another time, one of the Servants, whose Office it was to
fill my Trough every third Day with fresh Water; was so
careless to let a huge Frog (not perceiving it) slip out of his

Pail. The Frog lay concealed till I was put into my Boat, but then seeing a resting Place, climbed up, and made it lean so much on one Side, that I was forced to balance it with all my Weight on the other, to prevent overturning. When the Frog was got in, it hopped at once half the Length of the Boat, and then over my Head, backwards and forwards, dawbing my Face and Cloaths with its odious Slime. The Largeness of its Features made it appear the most deformed Animal that can be conceived. However, I desired *Glumdalclitch* to let me deal with it alone. I banged it a good while with one of my Sculls, and at last forced it to leap out of the Boat.

But, the greatest Danger I ever underwent in that Kingdom, was from a Monkey, who belonged to one of the Clerks of the Kitchen. *Glumdalclitch* had locked me up in her Closet, while she went somewhere upon Business, or a Visit. The Weather being very warm, the Closet Window was left open, as well as the Windows and the Door of my bigger Box, in which I usually lived, because of its Largeness and Conveniency. As I sat quietly meditating at my Table, I heard something bounce in at the Closet Window, and skip about from one Side to the other ; whereat, although I were much alarmed, yet I ventured to look out, but not stirring from my Seat ; and then I saw this frolicksome Animal, frisking and leaping up and down, till at last he came to my Box, which he seemed to view with great Pleasure and Curiosity, peeping in at the Door and every Window. I retreated to the farther Corner of my Room, or Box ; but the Monkey looking in at every Side, put me into such a Fright, that I wanted Presence of Mind to conceal my self under the Bed, as I might easily have done. After some time spent in peeping, grinning, and chattering, he at last espyed me ; and reaching one of his Paws in at the Door, as a Cat does when she plays with a Mouse, although I often shifted Place to avoid him ; he at length seized the Lappet of my Coat (which being made of that Country Silk, was very thick and strong) and dragged me out. He took me up in his right Fore-foot, and held me. When I offered to struggle, he squeezed me so hard, that I thought it more prudent to submit. I have good Reason to believe that he took me for a young one of his own Species, by his often stroaking my Face very gently with his other Paw. In these Diversions he was interrupted by a Noise at the Closet Door, as if some Body were opening it; whereupon he suddenly leaped up to the Window at which he had come in, and thence upon the Leads and Gutters, walking upon three Legs, and holding me in the fourth, till he clambered up to a Roof that was next to ours. I heard *Glumdalclitch* give a Shriek at the Moment he was carrying me out. The poor Girl was almost distracted: That Quarter of the Palace was all in an Uproar; the Servants ran for Ladders; the Monkey was seen by Hundreds in the Court, sitting upon the Ridge of a Building, holding me like a Baby in one of his Fore-Paws. Some of the People threw up Stones, hoping to drive the Monkey down; but this was strictly forbidden, or else very probably my Brains had been dashed out.

The Ladders were now applied, and mounted by several Men; which the Monkey observing, and finding himself almost encompassed; not being able to make Speed enough with his three Legs, let me drop on a Ridge-Tyle, and made his Escape. Here I sat for some time five Hundred Yards from the Ground, expecting every Moment to be blown down by the Wind, or to fall by my own Giddiness, and come tumbling over and over from the Ridge to the Eves. But an honest Lad, one of my Nurse's Footmen, climbed up, and putting me into his Breeches Pocket, brought me down safe.

CHAPTER SIX

SEVERAL CONTRIVANCES OF THE AUTHOR TO PLEASE THE KING AND
QUEEN. HE SHEWS HIS SKILL IN MUSICK.

I USED to attend the King's Levee once or twice a Week, and had often seen him under the Barber's Hand, which indeed was at first very terrible to behold. For, the Razor was almost twice as long as an ordinary Scythe. His Majesty, according to the Custom of the Country, was only shaved twice a Week. I once prevailed on the Barber to give me some of the Suds and Lather, out of which I picked Forty or Fifty of the

strongest Stumps of Hair, I then took a Piece of fine Wood, and
cut it like the Back of Comb, making several Holes in it at
equal Distance, with as small a Needle as I could get from
Glumdalclitch. I fixed in the Stumps so artificially, scraping
and sloping them with my Knife towards the Points, that I
made a very tolerable Comb ; which was a seasonable Supply,
my own being so much broken in the Teeth, that it was almost
useless : Neither did I know any Artist in that Country so nice
and exact, as would undertake to make me another.

And this puts me in mind of an Amusement wherein I spent
many of my leisure Hours. I desired the Queen's Woman to
save for me the Combings of her Majesty's Hair, whereof in
time I got a good Quantity ; and consulting with my Friend
the Cabinet-maker, who had received general Orders to do
little Jobbs for me ; I directed him to make two Chair-frames,
no larger than those I had in my Box, and then to bore little
Holes with a fine Awl round those Parts where I designed the
Backs and Seats ; through these Holes I wove the strongest
Hairs I could pick out, just after the Manner of Cane-chairs
in *England*. When they were finished, I made a Present of them
to her Majesty, who kept them in her Cabinet, and used to
shew them for Curiosities ; as indeed they were the Wonder
of every one who beheld them. The Queen would have had me
sit upon one of these Chairs, but I absolutely refused to obey
her; protesting I would rather dye a Thousand Deaths than
place a dishonourable Part of my Body on those precious
Hairs that once adorned her Majesty's Head. Of these Hairs
(as I had always a Mechanical Genius) I likewise made a neat
little Purse about five Foot long, with her Majesty's Name
decyphered in Gold Letters ; which I gave to *Glumdalclitch*,
by the Queen's Consent.

The King, who delighted in Musick, had frequent Consorts
at Court, to which I was sometimes carried, and set in my Box
on a Table to hear them : But, the Noise was so great, that I
could hardly distinguish the Tunes. I am confident, that all
the Drums and Trumpets of a Royal Army, beating and sound-
ing together just at your Ears, could not equal it. My Practice
was to have my Box removed from the Places where the
Performers sat, as far as I could ; then to shut the Doors and

Windows of it, and draw the Window-Curtains; after which I found their Musick not disagreeable.

I had learned in my Youth to play a little upon the Spinet; *Glumdalclitch* kept one in her Chamber, and a Master attended twice a Week to teach her: I call it a Spinet, because it somewhat resembled that Instrument, and was play'd upon in the same Manner. A Fancy came into my Head, that I would entertain the King and Queen with an *English* Tune upon this Instrument. But this appeared extremely difficult: For, the Spinet was near sixty Foot long, each Key being almost a Foot wide; so that, with my Arms extended. I could not reach to above five Keys; and to press them down required a good smart stroak with my Fist, which would be too great a Labour, and to no purpose. The Method I contrived was this. I prepared two round Sticks about the Bigness of common Cudgels; they were thicker at one End than the other; and I covered the thicker End with a Piece of a Mouse's Skin, that by rapping on them, I might neither Damage the Tops of the Keys, nor interrupt the Sound. Before the Spinet, a Bench was placed about four Foot below the Keys, and I was put upon the Bench. I ran sideling upon it that way and this, as fast as I could, banging the proper Keys with my two Sticks; and made a shift to play a Jigg to the great Satisfaction of both their Majesties.

CHAPTER SEVEN

THE KING AND QUEEN MAKE A PROGRESS TO THE FRONTIERS. THE AUTHOR ATTENDS THEM. THE MANNER IN WHICH HE LEAVES THE COUNTRY VERY PARTICULARLY RELATED. HE RETURNS TO ENGLAND.

I HAD always a strong Impulse that I should some time recover my Liberty, although it were impossible to conjecture by what Means, or to form any Project with the least Hope of succeeding. The Ship in which I sailed was the first ever known to be driven within Sight of that Coast; and the King had given strict Orders, that if at any Time another appeared, it should be taken ashore, and with all its Crew and Passengers brought in a Tumbril to *Lorbrulgrud*. I was indeed treated with much Kindness; I was the Favourite of a great King and Queen, and the Delight of the whole Court; but it was upon such a Foot as ill became the Dignity of human Kind. I could never forget those domestick Pledges I had left behind me. I wanted to be among People with whom I could converse upon even Terms; and walk about the Streets and Fields without Fear of being trod to Death like a Frog or young Puppy. But, my Deliverance came sooner than I expected, and in a Manner not very common: The whole Story and Circumstances of which I shall faithfully relate.

I had now been two Years in this Country; and, about the Beginning of the third, *Glumdalclitch* and I attended the King and Queen in Progress to the South Coast of the Kingdom. I was carried as usual in my Travelling-Box, which, as I have already described, was a very convenient Closet of twelve Foot wide. I had ordered a Hammock to be fixed by silken Ropes from the four Corners at the Top; to break the Jolts, when a Servant carried me before him on Horseback, as I sometimes desired; and would often sleep in my Hammock while we were upon the Road. On the Roof of my Closet, set not directly over the Middle of the Hammock, I ordered the Joiner to cut out a Hole of a Foot square to give me Air in hot Weather as I slept; which Hole I shut at pleasure with a Board that drew backwards and forwards through a Groove.

When we came to our Journey's End, the King thought proper to pass a few Days at a Palace he hath near *Flanflasnic*, a City within eighteen *English* Miles of the Sea-side. *Glumdalclitch* and I were much fatigued: I had gotten a small Cold; but the poor Girl was so ill as to be confined to her Chamber. I longed to see the Ocean, which must be the only Scene of my Escape, if ever it should happen. I pretended to be worse than I really was; and desired leave to take the fresh Air of the Sea, with a Page whom I was very fond of, and who had sometimes been trusted with me. I shall never forget with what Unwillingness *Glumdalclitch* consented; nor the strict Charge she gave the Page to be careful of me; bursting at the same time into a Flood of Tears, as if she had some

Foreboding of what was to happen. The Boy took me out in my Box about Half an Hour's Walk from the Palace, towards the Rocks on the Sea-Shore. I ordered him to set me down; and lifting up one of my Sashes, cast many a wistful melancholy Look towards the Sea. I found myself not very well; and told the Page that I had a Mind to take a Nap in my Hammock, which I hoped would do me good. I got in, and the Boy shut the Window close down, to keep out the Cold. I soon fell asleep: And all I can conjecture is, that while I slept, the Page, thinking no Danger could happen, went among the Rocks to look for Birds Eggs. I found my self suddenly awaked with a violent Pull upon the Ring which was fastned at the Top of my Box for the Conveniency of Carriage. I felt the Box raised very high in the Air, and then born forward with prodigious Speed. The first Jolt had like to have shaken me out of my Hammock; but afterwards the Motion was easy enough. I called out several times as loud as I could raise my Voice, but all to no purpose. I looked towards my Windows, and could see nothing but the Clouds and Sky. I heard a Noise just over my Head like the clapping of Wings; and then began to perceive the woeful Condition I was in; that some Eagle had got the Ring of my Box in his Beak, with an Intent to let it fall on a Rock, like a Tortoise in a Shell, and then pick out my Body and devour it. For the Sagacity and Smell of this Bird enable him to discover his Quarry at a great Distance, although better concealed than I could be within a two Inch Board.

In a little time I observed the Noise and flutter of Wings to encrease very fast; and my Box was tossed up and down like a Sign-post in a windy Day. I heard several Bangs or Buffets, as I thought, given to the Eagle (for such I am certain it must have been that held the Ring of my Box in his Beak) and then all on a sudden felt my self falling perpendicularly down for above a Minute; but with such incredible Swiftness that I almost lost my Breath. My Fall was stopped by a terrible Squash, that sounded louder to my Ears than the Cataract of *Niagara*; after which I was quite in the Dark for another Minute, and then my Box began to rise so high that I could see Light from the Tops of my Windows. I now perceived that I was fallen into the Sea. My Box, by the Weight of my

Body, the Goods that were in, and the broad Plates of Iron fixed for Strength at the four Corners of the Top and Bottom, floated about five Foot deep in Water. I did then, and do now suppose, that the Eagle which flew away with my Box was pursued by two or three others, and forced to let me drop while he was defending himself against the Rest, who hoped to share in the Prey. The Plates of Iron fastned at the Bottom of the Box, (for those were the strongest) preserved the Balance while it fell; and hindred it from being broken on the Surface of the Water. Every Joint of it was well grooved, and the Door did not move on Hinges, but up and down like a Sash; which kept my Closet so tight that very little Water came in. I got with much Difficulty out of my Hammock, having first ventured to draw back the Slip board on the Roof already mentioned contrived on purpose to let in Air; for want of which I found my self almost stifled.

How often did I then wish my self with my dear *Glumdalclitch*, from whom one single Hour had so far divided me! And I may say with Truth, that in the midst of my own Misfortune, I could not forbear lamenting my poor Nurse, the Grief she would suffer for my Loss, the Displeasure of the Queen, and the Ruin of her Fortune. Perhaps many Travellers have not been under greater Difficulties and Distress than I was at this Juncture; expecting every Moment to see my Box dashed in Pieces, or at least overset by the first violent Blast, or a rising Wave. A Breach in one single Pane of Glass would have been immediate Death: Nor could any thing have preserved the Windows but the strong Lattice Wires placed on the outside against Accidents in Travelling. I saw the Water ooze in at several Crannies, although the Leaks were not considerable; and I endeavoured to stop them as well as I could. I was not able to lift up the Roof of my Closet, which otherwise I certainly should have done, and sat on the Top of it, where I might at least preserve myself from being shut up, as I may call it, in the Hold. Or, if I escaped these Dangers for a Day or two, what could I expect but a miserable Death of Cold and Hunger! I was four Hours under these Circumstances, expecting and indeed wishing every Moment to be my last.

I have already told the Reader, that there were two strong

Staples fixed upon the Side of my Box which had no Window, and into which the Servant, who used to carry me on Horseback, would put a Leathern Belt, and buckle it about his Waist. Being in this disconsolate State, I heard, or at least thought I I heard some kind of grating Noise on that Side of my Box where the Staples were fixed; and soon after I began to fancy that the Box, was pulled, or towed along in the Sea; for I now and then felt a sort of tugging, which made the Waves rise near the Tops of my Windows, leaving me almost in the Dark. This gave me some faint Hopes of Relief, although I were not able to imagine how it could be brought about. I ventured to unscrew one of my Chairs, which were always fastned to the Floor; and having made a hard shift to screw it down again directly under the Slipping-board that I had lately opened; I mounted on the Chair, and putting my Mouth as near as I could to the Hole, I called for Help in a loud Voice, and in all the Languages I understood. I then fastned my Handkerchief to a Stick I usually carried, and thrusting it up the Hole, I waved it several times in the Air; that if any Boat or Ship were near, the Seamen might conjecture some unhappy Mortal to be shut up in the Box.

I found no Effect from all I could do, but plainly perceived my Closet to be moved along; and in the Space of an Hour, or better, that Side of the Box where the Staples were, and had no Window, struck against something that was hard. I apprehended it to be a Rock, and found my self tossed more than ever. I plainly heard a Noise upon the Cover of my Closet, like that of a Cable, and the grating of it as it passed through the Ring. I then found my self hoisted up by Degrees at least three Foot higher than I was before. Whereupon, I again thrust up my Stick and Handkerchief, calling for Help till I was almost hoarse. In return to which, I heard a great Shout repeated three times, giving me such Transports of Joy as are not to be conceived but by those who feel them. I now heard a trampling over my Head; and somebody calling through the Hole with a loud Voice in the *English* Tongue: *If there be any Body below, let them speak.* I answered, I was an *Englishman*, drawn by ill Fortune into the greatest Calamity that ever any Creature underwent; and begged, by all that was moving, to be delivered out of the Dungeon I was in. The Voice replied, I was safe, for my Box was fastned to their Ship; and the Carpenter should immediately come, and saw an Hole in the Cover, large enough to pull me out. I answered, that was needless, and would take up too much Time; for there was no more to be done, but let one of the Crew put his Finger into the Ring, and take the Box out of the Sea into the Ship, and so into the Captain's Cabbin. Some of them upon hearing me talk so wildly, thought I was mad; others laughed; for indeed it never came into my Head, that I was now got among People of my own Stature and Strength. The Carpenter came, and in a few Minutes sawed a Passage about four Foot square; then let down a small Ladder, upon which I mounted, and from thence was taken into the Ship in a very weak Condition.

The Sailors were all in Amazement, and asked me a thousand Questions, which I had no Inclination to answer. I was equally confounded at the Sight of so many Pigmies; for such I took them to be, after having so long accustomed my Eyes to the monstrous Objects I had left. But the Captain, Mr. *Thomas Wilcocks*, an honest worthy *Shropshire* Man, observing I was ready to faint, took me into his Cabbin, gave me a Cordial to comfort me, and made me *turn in* upon his own Bed; advising me to take a little Rest, of which I had great need. Before I went to sleep I gave him to understand, that I had some valuable Furniture in my Box too good to be lost; a fine Hammock, an handsome Field-Bed, two Chairs, a Table and a Cabinet: That my Closet was hung on all Sides, or rather quilted with Silk and Cotton: That if he would let one of the Crew bring my Closet into his Cabbin, I would open it before him, and shew him my Goods. The Captain hearing me utter these Absurdities, concluded I was raving: However, (I suppose to pacify me) he promised to give Order as I desired; and going upon Deck, sent some of his Men down into my Closet, from whence (as I afterwards found) they drew up all my Goods, and stripped off the Quilting; but the Chairs, Cabinet and Bedsted being screwed to the Floor, were damaged by the Ignorance of the Seamen, who tore them up by Force. Then they knocked off some of the Boards for the Use of the Ship; and when they had got all they had a Mind for, let the Hulk drop into the Sea,

which by Reason of many Breaches made in the Bottom and
Sides, sunk *to rights*. And indeed I was glad not to have been
a Spectator of the Havock they made ; because I am confident
it would have sensibly touched me, by bringing former Passages
into my Mind, which I had rather forget.

I slept some Hours, but perpetually disturbed with Dreams
of the Place I had left, and the Dangers I had escaped. However,
upon waking I found my self much recovered. It was now
about eight a Clock at Night, and the Captain ordered Supper
immediately, thinking I had already fasted too long. He
entertained me with great Kindness, observing me not to look
wildly, or talk inconsistently ; and when we were left alone,
desired I would give him a Relation of my Travels, and by
what Accident I came to be set adrift in that monstrous wooden
Chest. He said, that about twelve a Clock at Noon, as he was
looking through his Glass, he spied it at a Distance, and thought
it was a Sail, which he had a Mind to make ; being not much
out of his Course, in hopes of buying some Biscuit, his own
beginning to fall short. That, upon coming nearer, and finding
his Error, he sent out his Long-boat to discover what I was ;
that his Men came back in a Fright, swearing they had seen a
swimming House. That he laughed at their Folly, and went
himself in the Boat, ordering his Men to take a strong Cable
along with them. That the Weather being calm, he rowed
round me several times, observed my Windows, and the Wire
Lattices that defended them. That he discovered two Staples
upon one Side, which was all of Boards, without any Passage
for Light. He then commanded his Men to row up to that
Side ; and fastning a Cable to one of the Staples, ordered his
Men to tow my Chest (as he called it) towards the Ship. When
it was there, he gave Directions to fasten another Cable to the
Ring fixed in the Cover, and to raise up my Chest with Pullies,
which all the Sailors were not able to do above two or three
Foot. He said, they saw my Stick and Handkerchief thrust
out of the Hole, and concluded, that some unhappy Man must
be shut up in the Cavity. I asked whether he or the Crew had
seen any prodigious Birds in the Air about the Time he first
discovered me : To which he answered, that discoursing this
Matter with the Sailors while I was asleep, one of them said

he had *observed* three Eagles flying towards the North; but remarked nothing of their being larger than the usual Size; which I suppose must be imputed to the great Height they were at: And he could not guess the Reason of my Question. I then asked the Captain how far he reckoned we might be from Land; he said, by the best Computation he could make, we were at least an hundred Leagues. I assured him, that he must be mistaken by almost half; for I had not left the Country from whence I came, above two Hours before I dropt into the Sea. Whereupon he began again to think that my Brain was disturbed, of which he gave me a Hint, and advised me to go to Bed in a Cabin he had provided. I assured him I was well refreshed with his good Entertainment and Company, and as much in my Senses as ever I was in my Life. He then grew serious, and desired to ask me freely whether I were not troubled in Mind by the Consciousness of some enormous Crime, for which I was punished at the Command of some Prince, by exposing me in that Chest; as great Criminals in other Countries have been forced to Sea in a leaky Vessel without Provisions: For, although he should be sorry to have taken so ill a Man into his Ship, yet he would engage his Word to set me safe on Shore in the first Port where we arrived. He added, that his Suspicions were much increased by some very absurd Speeches I had delivered at first to the Sailors, and afterwards to himself, in relation to my Closet or Chest, as well as by my odd Looks and Behaviour while I was at Supper.

I begged his Patience to hear me tell my Story; which I faithfully did from the last Time I left *England*, to the Moment he first discovered me. And, as Truth always forceth its Way into rational Minds; so, this honest worthy Gentleman, who had some Tincture of Learning, and very good Sense, was immediately convinced of my Candor and Veracity. But, further to confirm all I had said, I entreated him to give Order that my Cabinet should be brought, of which I kept the Key in my Pocket, (for he had already informed me how the Seamen disposed of my Closet) I opened it in his Presence, and shewed him the small Collection of Rarities I made in the Country from whence I had been so strangely delivered. There was the

Comb I had contrived out of the Stumps of the King's Beard ; and another of the same Materials, but fixed into a paring of her Majesty's Thumb-nail, which served for the Back. There was a Collection of Needles and Pins from a Foot to half a Yard long. Four Wasp-Stings, like Joyners Tacks : Some Combings of the Queen's Hair : A Gold Ring which one Day she made me a Present of in a most obliging Manner, taking it from her little Finger, and throwing it over my Head like a Collar. I desired the Captain would please to accept this Ring in Return of his Civilities ; which he absolutely refused. I shewed him a Corn that I had cut off with my own Hand from a Maid of Honour's Toe ; it was about the Bigness of a *Kentish* Pippin, and grown so hard, that when I returned to *England*, I got it hollowed into a Cup and set in Silver. Lastly, I desired him to see the Breeches I had then on, which were made of a Mouse's Skin.

I could force nothing on him but a Footman's Tooth, which I observed him to examine with great Curiosity, and found he had a Fancy for it. He received it with abundance of Thanks, more than such a Trifle could deserve. It was drawn by an unskilful Surgeon in a Mistake from one of *Glumdalclitch's* Men, who was afflicted with the Tooth-ach ; but it was as sound as any in his Head. I got it cleaned, and put it into my Cabinet. It was about a Foot long, and four Inches in Diameter.

The Captain was very well satisfied with this plain Relation I had given him ; and said, he hoped when we returned to *England*, I would oblige the World by putting it in Paper, and making it publick. He said, he wondered at one Thing very much; which was, to hear me speak so loud ; asking me whether the King or Queen of that Country were thick of Hearing. I told him it was what I had been used to for above two Years past; and that I admired as much at the Voices of him and his Men, who seemed to me only to whisper, and yet I could hear them well enough. But, when I spoke in that Country, it was like a Man talking in the Street to another looking out from the Top of a Steeple, unless when I was placed on a Table, or held in any Person's Hand. I told him, I had likewise observed another Thing ; that when I first got into the Ship, and the Sailors stood all about me, I thought they were the most little contemptible Creatures I had ever beheld. For, indeed, while I was in that Prince's Country, I could never endure to look in a Glass after my Eyes had been accustomed to such prodigious Objects; because the Comparison gave me so despicable a Conceit of my self. The Captain said, that while we were at Supper, he observed me to look at every thing with a Sort of Wonder; and that I often seemed hardly able to contain my Laughter; which he knew not well how to take, but imputed it to some Disorder in my Brain. I answered, it was very true; and I wondered how I could forbear, when I saw his Dishes of the Size of a Silver Three-pence, a Leg of Pork hardly a Mouthful, a Cup not so big as a Nutshell: And so I went on, describing the rest of his Household stuff and Provisions after the same Manner. For although the Queen had ordered a little Equipage of all Things necessary for me while I was in her Service; yet my Ideas were wholly taken up with what I saw on every Side of me; and I winked at my own Littleness, as People do at their own Faults. The Captain understood my Raillery very well, and merrily replied with the old *English* Proverb, that he doubted, my Eyes were bigger than my Belly; for he did not observe my Stomach so good, although I had fasted all Day: And continuing his Mirth, protested he would have gladly given an Hundred Pounds to have seen my Closet in the Eagle's Bill, and afterwards in its Fall from so great an Height into the Sea; which would certainly have been a most astonishing Object, worthy to have the Description of it transmitted to future Ages.

The Captain having been at *Tonquin*, was in his Return to *England* driven North Eastward to the Latitude of 44 Degrees, and of Longitude 143. But meeting a Trade Wind two Days after I came on board him, we sailed Southward a long Time, and coasting *New-Holland*, kept our Course West-south-west, and then South-south-west till we doubled the *Cape of Good-hope*. Our Voyage was very prosperous, but I shall not trouble the Reader with a Journal of it. The Captain called in at one or two Ports, and sent in his Longboat for Provisions and fresh Water; but I never went out of the Ship till we came into the *Downs*, which was on the 3d Day of *June* 1706, about nine Months after my Escape. I offered to leave my Goods in

Security for Payment of my Freight; but the Captain protested
he would not receive one Farthing. We took kind Leave of
each other; and I made him promise he would come to see
me at my House in *Redriff*. I hired a Horse and Guide for five
Shillings, which I borrowed of the Captain.

As I was on the Road; observing the Littleness of the Houses,
the Trees, the Cattle and the People, I began to think my self
in *Lilliput*. I was afraid of trampling on every Traveller I met;
and often called aloud to have them stand out of the Way; so
that I had like to have gotten one or two broken Heads for my
Impertinence.

When I came to my own House, for which I was forced to
enquire, one of the Servants opening the Door, I bent down to
go in (like a Goose under a Gate) for fear of striking my Head.
My Wife ran out to embrace me, but I stooped lower than her
Knees, thinking she could otherwise never be able to reach my
Mouth. My Daughter kneeled to ask me Blessing, but I could
not see her till she arose; having been so long used to stand
with my Head and Eyes erect to above Sixty Foot; and then
I went to take her up with one Hand, by the Waist. I looked
down upon the Servants, and one or two Friends who were
in the House, as if they had been Pigmies, and I a Giant. I told
my Wife, she had been too thrifty; for I found she had starved
herself and her Daughter to nothing. In short, I behaved my
self so unaccountably, that they were all of the Captain's
Opinion when he first saw me; and concluded I had lost my
Wits. This I mention as an Instance of the great Power of
Habit and Prejudice.

In a little Time I and my Family and Friends came to a
right Understanding: But my Wife protested I should never
go to Sea any more; although my evil Destiny so ordered, that
she had not Power to hinder me; as the Reader may know
hereafter. In the mean Time, I here conclude the second
Part of my unfortunate Voyages.